Harlequin Romances

OTHER

Harlequin Romances

by SUE PETERS

Many of these titles are available at your local bookseller,
or through the Harlequin Reader Service.

For a free catalogue listing all available Harlequin Romances,
send your name and address to:

HARLEQUIN READER SERVICE,
M.P.O. Box 707, Niagara Falls, N.Y. 14302
Canadian address: Stratford, Ontario, Canada N5A 6W4

or use coupon at back of books.

One Special Rose

by

SUE PETERS

Harlequin Books

TORONTO • LONDON • NEW YORK • AMSTERDAM • SYDNEY • WINNIPEG

Original hardcover edition published in 1976
by Mills & Boon Limited

ISBN 0-373-02030-9

Harlequin edition published December 1976

Printed in Canada

CHAPTER ONE

It was a lovely morning.

The sort of morning, thought Pip, shifting her seat on the top of the five-barred gate to avoid a persistent splinter that made its presence felt through the soft, ribbed corduroy of her working trousers, the sort of morning that seemed to have strayed from the coming summer, and wandered backwards in time to settle like a bright butterfly on the bare branches of March.

The sun had an unseasonal strength, and she pushed up the vivid blue sleeves of her chunky Fair Isle sweater, relishing the feel of the rays against her bare arms that had been too long encased in similar clothing as a protection against a winter as harsh as any her own northern home county could produce. She had always understood the southern winters were kinder, but the six months she had been at the Shieldon Nurseries had disabused her of that particular theory.

"Even the burn's frozen over!" she had exclaimed on New Year's morning, unable to hide her surprise as she viewed the narrow stream that fed the Monks' Pool, and was now reduced to a trickle in the middle that looked as if it, too, would soon disappear under the crinkling ice that coated each side with a rapidly thickening cover.

"We call them streams down here." Giles Shieldon appeared behind her, and his voice was as crisp as the morning that was rapidly turning Pip's nose a similar shade to the sweater she wore, the same one that she had got on now. There wasn't much of her face below her nose left visible, for she had turned up the polo collar of her woolly in order to protect her ears, which were ill covered by the short cut of her fair, curly hair that clung as close to her head as a boy's.

It isn't everyone whose nose matches their eyes, she thought ruefully, ducking that blue member further into the knitted ribbing of the collar, and sticking her hands deep into her slacks pockets in an effort to bring back some feeling into her numbed fingers. She wondered, not for the first time, why it was that her new boss should always manage to arrive in time to correct her for mistakes, real or supposed, a habit that was beginning to get on her nerves no matter how hard she tried not to let it.

New Year's Day wasn't the time to criticise people, she thought sourly, it was a time for celebrating. Her Border upbringing rose in protest at the calm indifference of these southern folk to such an important occasion, and she wondered fleetingly if Giles Shieldon's sharpness had its origin in an over-enthusiastic celebration the night before. She eyed him covertly as she directed her steps beside his along the wide, gravelled path that led towards the array of glasshouses and sheds that formed the workshops of the nursery, for although it was called the Shieldon Rose Nurseries, it also had a large general side – the bread and butter side, the senior foreman called it descriptively – from which Pip drew her daily requirements of material to perform her own particular function.

He didn't look as if he had celebrated the New Year at all, let alone too well. His brown eyes, that bent down on her a look as keen as the temperature out of doors, and about as friendly, she thought ruefully, were as clear and alert as on any ordinary morning; his skin was too brown with its constant exposure to the open air to tell whether he was pale underneath his tan or not, but his stride was as springy as it had been ever since she had known him, when she first came for an interview for the post loosely described as "florist" at the end of the summer last year.

"I advertised for someone with experience," the owner of the Shieldon Rose Nurseries told her with a blunt lack of encouragement when she presented herself in his office at the behest of his rather curt letter answering her application. His brown eyes raked impersonally over her slight figure in the bottle green suit with the pert cap to match that sat on her fair curls cheekily askew, declining to contain them all, so that a few escaped and curled up round the edge as if determined not to be denied a look at the outside world.

Pip flushed, her fair skin betraying the quick spark that showed in her deep blue eyes, that were shaded by the peak of her cap.

"I'm twenty-five," she forestalled his obvious question; it was one she had heard dozens of times before, and she had only to look in the mirror to realise that it was a mistake for which any stranger might be forgiven, for the glass gave back a reflection that looked to be scarcely twenty, let alone five years older. "I've been at Grenvilles for seven years, ever since I left school," she mentioned a nationally known firm of florists, one of the largest in the trade. "I took my training there, and I've been through every practical aspect of the business since." The administrative side didn't interest her; Pip loved growing things and determined that her work would remain among the flowers and plants that had become her life by now, and not among the impersonal statistics and paper work of an office, although her previous employer had offered her a lucrative position in that sphere more than once.

"With your knowledge you'd find it child's play," he coaxed, tempting her with a salary that made her gasp. She suspected it did her employer, too, but his offer was a measure of his keenness to retain her services. She refused it, unable to explain to him that paper didn't shine in the changing light as did a smooth green leaf, nor shade from bronze to cream all in one small petal, as when you looked

7

deep into the heart of an autumn chrysanthemum. Paper was dead stuff in your fingers, the typed word a cold unreality in contrast to the vibrant feel of firm green stems, and the soft clinging fronds of the variegated ivies that despite her skill always seemed more determined to twine round her busy fingers than to bind the particular piece of work upon which she was engaged.

Some of her work was on paper, of course, for her job at Grenvilles, and again at the Shieldon Rose Nurseries, entailed more than that of an ordinary florist, including organising displays for large functions, and such things as the County Shows, and other major out-of-doors events, which provided a useful display ground for the more versatile firms, and a valuable advertisement of their capabilities. Such shows needed a good deal of planning, most of which had to be on paper at first, but it was different working out the displays like this herself, visualising the backgrounds against which she had to achieve her various effects, and what those effects were to be, as well as how to achieve them from the materials the nursery could provide, then finally supervising the handling of these materials by the nursery staff.

The staff had resented working for her at first, regarding her youthful appearance with openly expressed doubts, but after her handling of the first big show, for which Shieldons received a coveted cup, a much publicised commendation, and a boomerang of new orders as a result, they had accepted her skill and forgot her appearance beyond an approving comment now and then, and she now had no lack of volunteers when she was doing outside work, as it was called in the jargon of the nursery. The staff had accepted her, but Giles Shieldon had not, reflected Pip, easing her position on the top of the gate to feel in her trousers pocket for the chocolate bar that Betsy 'Odgetts had given her for elevenses.

"Pop it in your pocket, lovie," she pressed it into Pip's hand, "it'll stop the grubs biting until you get back."

Pip took it, more to please her motherly little landlady than for any other reason, but suddenly the top of a five-barred gate in the unexpectedly warm sunshine seemed a good place to sit and eat a chocolate bar, and think about the last six months, and her prospects in her new job. The long confinement in the warmth of her pocket had made the chocolate soft, and Pip peeled off the silver paper and licked the oozy bits from her fingers. She hadn't stopped for a break since six o'clock breakfast because she had wanted to get the particular job she was out on done in good time. It had been an awkward assignment, to decorate a suite of small, interconnecting rooms for a wedding party later that day. It had been difficult to decorate it effectively and still leave room for a multitude of guests to wander unhindered from the buffet reception through the various rooms and alcoves in which the wedding gifts had been displayed. She had never seen so many presents gathered together in one spot, she reflected, and wondered if the bride and groom realised how lucky they were. Probably not, from what she had gathered from the garrulous hotel chef who had got under her feet while he fussily arranged and rearranged his buffet, and hindered her from finishing her own floral decorations; both the bride and the groom were the only children of wealthy parents who indulged their every whim the moment it was uttered.

It was more fun to work for yourself, she thought. Her own parents weren't poor, they were both doctors in a joint practice in their home town, and they had passed on to Pip and her brother their own enormous enthusiasm for living, of which work was an inescapable part, to be entered into with zest, for a satisfaction that was a greater reward than its financial return. Her brother was studying to follow in his parents' footsteps, and Pip suspected that they secretly hoped she would do the same, but with the open-minded outlook which was part of them they let her train for the career she longed for, giving her generous encouragement, and hiding their own disappointment so that she was left with no feeling of guilt for letting them down.

There was a good view of the nursery from where she sat, she thought appreciatively. From her exalted perch she could see right across the top of the big green van that she had parked by the side of the lane. It had the nursery emblem emblazoned on its side, an upright shield etched in black, with a single deep gold rosebud obliquely across the face, and the words "Shieldon Rose Nurseries" in a neat, readable script underneath. Giles Shieldon had probably sketched out the emblem himself; certainly the writing was a replica of his own – she had seen it often enough on the instruction notes he was in the habit of leaving for her when he wanted her to deal with new orders. The man himself was a bit like his own emblem, she thought scathingly, upright and unyielding. One could almost imagine a motto in Latin tattooed indelibly across his back. Maybe it was tattooed on his mind, she thought with an inward grin. She had rarely seen him smile. Looking back, she realised that when he did it was always when he was with Skippy, her amiable landlady's small granddaughter.

"I'm 'Lisabeth really," explained the youngest sprig of the family when Pip arrived with her suitcases, "but everyone calls me Skippy. 'Less they're cross," she amended truthfully, "an' the vicar, he always says 'hello, Elisabeth,' and pats me on the head," she mimicked the village reverend in a laughable fashion, and grinned widely at Pip's amused chuckle. "He knows 'cos he christened me," she excused him.

"I know, it's awkward being called two names," Pip smiled at her with ready sympathy, and received the reaction she was accustomed to from children and animals, who invariably responded to her warmhearted friendliness. "Everybody calls me Pip, but my name's Philippa, really," she told her small companion conspiratorially, wondering as she always did why her family had bothered.

"We'll stick to Pip while you're with us, it's less of a mouthful." Giles Shieldon ducked under the doorway and swung Skippy out of the circle of Pip's arms, and up on to his shoulder. "Come and let's find a bunch of flowers for your gran, for the weekend." Over the months she had been at the nursery Pip discovered this was a Saturday morning ritual that the owner seemed to enjoy as much as the child, for he reported promptly at the kitchen doorway each weekend after breakfast to collect Skippy, and an hour later she reappeared bearing a mixed bunch of the best blooms the nursery had to offer, and joyfully carrying in her jeans pocket a silver coin as her pocket money.

"You spoil her, Mister Giles," Betsy invariably protested, but her rosy face beamed with pleasure at her own bouquet, and her honest pride in her only grandchild.

Skippy caused Pip to wonder for a while, but the appearance of her widowed mother at the weekends solved the mystery, she worked in a nearby town during the week to support herself and the child, and returned to her parents at the weekend, cheerfully lending a pair of capable hands to whatever task turned up around the house.

From where she sat Pip could pick out the cottage easily enough. It was hardly the word for it really, she reflected, but it was difficult to know what to call a converted monastery, of which the cottage was only a part. Betsy had recounted its history to her one evening when they sat round the fire toasting themselves after a particularly hectic day, sleepily glad of the warmth and the feeling of security behind doors tightly shut against the storm outside. It had been a storm that was not only of nature's making, either, she thought gloomily. She had put her foot into it well and truly with her employer, by making a perfectly innocent remark in answer to a stranger, whose question she had no possible means of knowing was a barbed one.

She had been on her way from one of the greenhouses towards her own workshed when she met the man wandering along the gravel path, and stopped to ask him if she could help. The public weren't usually allowed this deep into the nursery, and after directing him to the selling section at the front – it was too big to be called a shop, and "store" didn't seem to fit into the background somehow – she walked back with him to make sure he didn't get lost. It was easy enough to lose oneself among the maze of glasshouses and potting sheds, as she had discovered when she first arrived, and she guessed the owner of the nurseries wouldn't appreciate strangers wandering about his own private grounds, which lay away from the nursery to one side, so she turned herself into a temporary guide, remarking on the weather to break the ice as one does to a casual stranger whom one does not expect to meet again.

"What a fine sight that tree makes!" The man paused in their wandering and regarded the bare arms of the huge elm tree standing stark against the wild sky.

"Yes, doesn't it?" Pip appreciated his point, but with a busy morning ahead of her she didn't want to stop and chat.

"I hear Shieldon's thinking of having it felled. Seems a pity," her companion remarked.

"Oh, what a shame!" Pip paused in her walk and had another look at the tree. "I wonder why he wants to do that? It seems a pity to get rid of it."

"So you think it's a pity to get rid of that elm, do you?" Giles Shieldon threw her remark back at her angrily just as she was brushing off her bench ready to lock up for the evening and go in to dinner.

"What do – oh, that one." Pip wasn't really interested in the elm, she was too hungry just now to think of much else except her meal, and for a moment or two she wondered what he meant, then she remembered her remark to the stranger on the path. "How did you . . . ?"

"I didn't, until now." Her employer thrust the evening paper in front of her nose with a furious gesture. "The local *Echo* just informed me," he told her bitingly, and turning on his heel he slammed the door to behind him. She could hear his footsteps ramming hard and firm on the gravel path outside, as clipped as his tone, and just as indicative of the state of his feelings. Pip took his paper, she had no option, he dumped it into her hands, and going back to her workbench she pulled the telescopic arm of the lamp closer to her and sat down again on her high stool, oddly thankful to take the weight off her legs that for some reason felt suddenly unsteady. She spread the copy of the *Echo* across the top of the worktable, and bent her eyes on the print emblazoned in bold black and white across the front page.

"Environmentalists find unexpected ally in fight to save elm tree. Member of nursery staff says it would be a pity to get rid of. . . ." There was a lot more in the same vein, most of it the usual mixture of uninformed emotionalism by people whose misdirected enthusiasm outstripped their factual knowledge.

"Of all the nerve!" Pip's cheeks went hot with indignation as she remembered her own naïve helpfulness to the stranger who she thought had lost his way. So he was a reporter, was he? "I wish I'd let him lose himself," she fumed. "I wish I'd let Giles find him." She could think of no worse fate for any trespasser, and crushed down a quick feeling of pity for the man when Giles did eventually meet up with him, as she had no doubt he intended to from the look on his face when he left her. Her own lost its rosy flush at the thought that she had to meet him herself in the morning to sort out the details of floral decorations for a big function that was to be held the following month in the largest hotel the nearby market town could boast.

"I want to go over the details with you. Oh, I shall want you to be there on the evening, as well," added Giles, mentioning the date casually, as a warning, thought Pip, not to get herself involved in any personal arrangements on that day. She had no doubt he would expect her to cancel them if she had. So far as he was concerned the nursery seemed to come first, and everything – and everyone – else a poor second, though struggling to be fair, Pip conceded that he drove himself just as hard as he drove everyone else, and there was no doubt that the nursery was a success. A small spark of pride in her own particular contribution coursed through her as she regarded the house and buildings lying maplike below her, small as models from where she sat at the side of the high-reaching lane that dipped sharply in the next half mile, to twist itself around the side of the nursery boundary, and provide a useful access to the main road junction further on.

The clear March sunshine glinted on the serried rows of glasshouses, each with a slanting, glass-covered cold frame running the full length on each side, providing useful space for cuttings, and at the same time precautionary distance between the huge glasshouses themselves, that by the very nature of their material were vulnerable, and if built too close together would be made even more so. The long rows of cold tunnels, high half-hoops of steel covered by thick agricultural type plastic sheeting, lay like elongated igloos further to one side, and beyond that again the square, flat acres of rose trees in which the nursery specialised. They must be a wonderful sight in June, thought Pip, and wondered apprehensively if she would still be with Shieldons in three months'. time. She would like to see the roses in full bloom, but her unfortunate habit of falling foul of Giles Shieldon almost every time she encountered him had made her doubt whether she would be able to stay the course. It seemed a pity, because she enjoyed her job, in fact she liked everything about the place except its owner. She had still got to see him about that function, he hadn't been able to spare the time the morning after she had spoken to the reporter, and there had been no opportunity in the few days since then. She supposed he would call her some time during the afternoon, and she leaned her elbows on her knees, balancing on the top bar of the gate, and relishing the peace around her while it lasted.

A ring-dove stuttered in a nearby tree, enhancing the silence rather than destroying it, and a blackbird dived across the lane, screaming abuse at some intruder in a nearby thicket. Maybe a prowling cat that had come too close to its nest. Sounds such as these must have been familiar to the monks who laid the first stones of the house that dreamed below her in the sunshine. Betsy had told her it had once been a monastery. That was centuries ago, of course, and the original inhabitants had long since departed.

"Disbanded, they did, when the troubles came." Betsy called all the uprisings of history "troubles"; it saved her from having to remember dates, and which one was which. "Mister Giles' family's been here ever since," she said simply, spanning several hundred years of occupation that stamped her employer's family as one of the oldest in the land.

Pip had taken to Giles Shieldon's home immediately, she had been inside his own part of the house several times when she was working with him on particular jobs, and the cottage where she lodged with Sam and Betsy 'Odgetts was an extension of the same building, and just as old. The place was L-shaped, Giles living in the main part, which was a two-storey structure that had been converted by previous generations of Shieldons into a comfortable family home, which still retained its own small chapel, a touch that pointed to its original isolation, before even the nearby village and its own lovely old church were built.

The short stroke of the L, that had been converted into a dwelling house, was at one time a stable block, as evidenced by the cobbled yard behind it, complete with a well populated dovecote whose gentle inhabitants provided Pip with murmurous company whenever she felt like escaping from the cheerful bustle of the cottage, and the chattering demands of Skippy, who attached herself to Pip like a small, auburn-haired leech whenever she returned to the house. With the support of daily help from the village to do the cleaning in both the houses, Betsy coped for Giles as well as for her husband, and cheerfully added two of the nursery staff to her ministrations, in the shape of Pip and the only other employed specialist in the nursery, Stella Garvey.

When she first arrived at Shieldons Pip hoped that she and Stella might become friends. They both had similar assignments, being acknowledged experts in their own particular fields, though Stella's was on more exotic lines than her own, Pip decided. Orchids were the other girl's speciality, and she alone handled them. They were not flowers that Pip particularly liked, and she gladly left them alone, preferring the simpler beauty of her own sphere of work, but nevertheless she felt disappointed. The rest of the female staff of the nursery were drawn from the village, most of them were married and regarded Shieldons as handy employment which saved them from travelling on the doubtful country bus service into the market town several miles away. Their work was more mundane, consisting of the pricking out, disbudding, packing and picking variety, and when hometime came they disappeared villagewards to their domestic duties, leaving Stella and Pip to return to their quarters. Stella only came to the cottage for her meals; she occupied a small flat further along the L of the building that was at one time a groom's quarters.

Pip's assumption that she and Stella would team up for an occasional outing in the evening went sadly awry, for

Stella made it plain to Pip when she first arrived that she resented her presence in the nursery at all, openly wondering why Shieldons required another specialist on the premises when she was there already, and leaving Pip with no illusions that she considered her an interloper. She did not even offer to show her around the nursery premises, that Pip would have regarded as a normal courtesy to any stranger, an assumption that Giles obviously shared, for after introducing the two girls he left them on their own, no doubt thinking that Stella would do the honours. She promptly deserted the newcomer as soon as Giles Shieldon was safely out of sight, and left her to be finally rescued by Skippy, who took her on a grand tour and seemed thereafter to regard Pip as her own special property.

I don't suppose Stella and I would have much in common anyway, she consoled herself. Stella was a bit like her own orchids, her blue-black hair and black eyes having a sultry, tropical quality about them, her creamy skin showing nothing of the healthy colour that tinted Pip's, and her tall, sinuous carriage hinting at an elegance in the ballrooms she so often seemed to frequent, if her glittering evening dresses and the suave escorts who called at her flat regularly were anything to go by. Pip was glad that she wasn't obliged to share the flat with Stella, and wondered that Giles seemed to have nothing to say about the late hours the other girl arrived home, sometimes several times a week, leaving her sleepy and irritable the next morning, and ill equipped for the busy day ahead. The fact that he never criticised her for this was evinced by her look of genuine surprise after one particularly late night in mid-week, when Pip, at Betsy's behest, entered her quarters and shook her awake, so that she could start packing her delicate blooms for a particularly early delivery that Pip knew had to catch the early train.

"Get up, Stella, do! You'll have Giles after you!" The

thought made her blanch, but it seemed to have no visible effect on the other girl, who yawned her way into her clothes, unhurriedly lit a cigarette, and followed Pip back to the cottage where she consumed a cup of coffee with the same deliberate lack of haste. Pip noticed she took it black, with three spoons of sugar, unlike her usual creamy drink, which pointed, along with the dark shadows under her eyes, to a hectic party the evening before.

"He won't bite," she drawled, a touch of lazy amusement lurking in her sultry eyes.

"Well, he does at me. Practically every time we meet," Pip confessed honestly, still uneasy in case he walked in as he sometimes did to see if Betsy wanted anything in the way of vegetables for the day's meals. Sam, Betsy's husband, worked in the nursery himself, and Giles made sure he kept his wife well supplied with all her needs.

"He knows better than to bite at me. At least, that sort of bite," Stella smiled significantly. "Most men do," she added, removing herself from her chair at last and strolling outside behind Pip to where the path divided to their respective workshops. She still didn't hurry. Pip watched her coolly amble on her way, nodding to Giles as he passed her on the path. She heard him greet Stella, heard his civil, "Have you got everything you want?" before he resumed his stride in her own direction, where he paused and addressed her briskly.

"Are you waiting for something, Pip?"

"No, I . . . no!" Pip compressed her lips and swung on her heel, fumbling in her pocket for the key to her door, sternly keeping her walk below the run that her legs longed to make, anything to get the good stout wood between herself and the piercing look that bored into her from behind her back. She never wasted a minute of her working day, and she strongly resented his tone, implying from its curtness that he thought she was dawdling, when in fact she would have been as early as usual getting to her job if it hadn't been for Stella, and he had not spoken a word of criticism to her.

"She can get herself out of bed the next time!" she vowed crossly, stung into ill-humour herself at the injustice of Giles' treatment, and sucked a finger where a too hasty movement had drawn blood against the wire she was using to bind snow-white lilies to the base shape of an Easter cross. Pip would have liked to go home for Easter, but the distance was too far for the short holiday, and with the seasonal flush of orders she did not feel justified in taking any more days to make it a whole week break, even if Giles would have agreed to her being away while they were so busy.

"I mustn't forget to buy an Easter egg for Skippy. I'll get one when I'm passing the shops," she murmured, tying a mental knot in her hanky, and using the small lace-edged square to wipe the last vestiges of chocolate from her fingers. It was time she went. She had been sat on the gate for a good ten minutes, her nether end told her that it was ten minutes too long. The wood was hard and the edge of it was sharp – and the van would have cooled down by now. She had stopped in the first place to roll up the radiator cowl cover; she had forgotten it when she started out first thing that morning, and the unexpected warmth of the day had made the engine steam, but it had been a pleasant break, she thought contentedly. The staff always had about ten minutes in the middle of the morning at the nursery, and the break time would be over by the time she got back, so she did not feel she was sneaking time off by stopping for her snack. She wriggled herself on to the edge of the top bar ready to jump to the ground, and felt the seat of her slacks resist her pull.

"Bother!" The splinter had dug into the soft material, and rather than risk tearing good slacks she eased herself back to her former position and bent her fingers to the task of easing it away from the corduroy. A car engine droned towards her up the hill, but intent on her task she took no notice until she had finally parted the rough wood from the threads of cloth.

"Got it!" She gave herself a push with the palms of her hands and jumped to the ground, a not inconsiderable distance from the high-swung gate for someone small in stature, and landed in an awkward heap on the uneven ground underneath.

"You're likely to break an ankle if you do things like that." A pair of hard brown hands pulled her to her feet, and immediately released her. "Has your van broken down?"

"No, it – er – " Confused, Pip found herself looking up into Giles' face. She had to crick her neck and squint against the sun, which was full in her eyes, and put her at a disadvantage. He stood watching her, silent, awaiting her answer, and she felt the angry colour mount her cheeks, her normal reaction now every time she came across her employer. "He's impossible!" she thought, vexed at her own confusion, furious with herself as much as with him. "Why can't I treat him the same as Stella does?" she wondered. "She gets away with it, and he doesn't snap at her." She saw his eyebrows quirk, and he made a slight, impatient movement that forced her into speech. "The radiator boiled," she told him flatly, "so I stopped to let it cool off for a minute or two."

"I don't suppose it would have run out of water for the short distance left to the nursery." His tone was uncompromising. "What did you do, leave the radiator cover down all morning?"

It should have been obvious what she had done, or not done, thought Pip crossly, without him rubbing it in. She was not usually so careless, she had never had it happen before. Why did it have to happen now, while Giles was around? she wondered. She was in his bad books quite enough as it was, what with the newspaper reporter and the elm tree. And she had still got to work out the details of that function with him. He was bound to say something to her about that then, and she was not looking forward to the interview.

"I'll put the radiator cap back on – I see you managed to remove it." He swung back suddenly, facing her, his eyes keen. "I hope you had the sense not to put your face over the opening when you took the cap off?" His eyes raked her skin, looking for signs of a scald.

"Of course I didn't!" she was stung into a sharp retort. "I've been driving for quite long enough to know better than that." What did he think she was, a learner? her expression said, though she bit back the actual words. After all, Giles was the owner of the nurseries, and she wanted to keep her job. She enjoyed the variety and wider experience it offered, and she didn't want to have to go back to Grenvilles and ask for her old job back, though she had no doubt that it would be gleefully offered. She met his eyes briefly, her own dark with vexation, and surprised a gleam in the man's brown gaze that made her pause. Was he laughing at her? His lips had a twitch which was the nearest thing she had seen to a smile on them since she came, except when he was with Skippy, when he seemed to become a different being. Her face must have mirrored her surprise, for the gleam vanished, and his tone when he spoke was curt.

"Maybe when you've finished looking at the scenery you'll follow me back. I want to see you immediately after lunch about that function next month." He didn't say he would like to see her, just that he wanted to. "There's no time to waste if we're to get the details properly organised. I don't want anything to go wrong."

His tone implied that if he didn't supervise the job, something might, and Pip's chin came up, her pride in her own capabilities stung. If she'd been sitting on the gate enjoying the scenery – he had obviously seen her as he drove along the lane – she had taken no more time than she was entitled to for a break. Less, come to that; she had started work well before seven that morning.

With compressed lips she swung round him and headed for her van, trying not to admit even to herself that she was glad he had returned the radiator cap to its place, it was stiff and she had had a struggle to remove it. She fished the ignition key out of her pocket and slotted it into place. The engine started easily, warm from its morning running, and she was strongly tempted to pull round Giles' van and leave him standing, but resisted the impulse and waited meekly behind him until he had slammed his own door shut and started up. It would have been nice, she reflected maliciously, if his engine had failed to start and she could offer him a tow back, but nothing so satisfactory happened, it never did in real life, and he moved away cleanly from the verge, glancing back once to see that she followed him, and escorted her back to the nursery gates – like, thought Pip with simmering resentment, like a truant being hauled back by a righteous headmaster, with the promise of an interview, and retribution, later in the afternoon.

CHAPTER TWO

"It's that chocolate bar. I didn't eat it until just now, and it's spoiled my appetite," Pip excused herself for leaving half her lunch, and refused the hearty ginger pudding which Betsy offered.

"Hmmm. You won't get far on a bite of chocolate." Betsy eyed her with motherly concern. "You're not sickening for something, are you?" She took the same line with her lodger as she did with Skippy.

"Of course not," Pip scoffed, thankful that this time she could tell the truth. "I'll do justice to your dinner tonight, don't worry." The interview with Giles would be over by then, she thought with relief, and she could relax. With the prospect of a telling off from Giles still in front of her, the last thing she wanted to do was to eat. And with the coming function to discuss, she didn't want to feel sleepy with food, either. On top of her other transgressions, she daren't let her attention roam when she was talking over the detailed arrangements with Giles. She shivered at the thought of what might happen if she forgot something important. "Let me know when Mr. Shieldon's finished his lunch, will you, Betsy?" she asked. "He wants to see me afterwards, to go over the details of a job together."

"He finished eating five minutes after he started," her rotund little landlady retorted. "What with trying to coax him to eat, and now you. . . ." She clucked her tongue disapprovingly.

"Maybe he doesn't like much in the middle of the day either." Pip used her employer's poor appetite as an excuse for her own, not very successfully, for her active life usually gave her a healthy enjoyment of her meals, and Betsy was well aware of this.

"Morning, middle day or evening, it's all the same with Master Giles, ever since . . . oh well, maybe things will get back to normal one day, and I must say I'll be right glad when they do." Betsy disappeared kitchenwards with the scarcely touched meal, and through the open door Pip saw her stir up the dog from the hearthrug with the soft toe of her slipper.

"Come on, Punch, you might as well have the meat and greens if they won't eat it."

"You'll make that dog fat, using him as a dustbin," Sam's voice came from somewhere in the corner out of sight.

"Not with Skippy around," Betsy's voice was amused. "She runs herself and the dog to rags most days, the only chance he gets for a rest is while the lass is at school. C'mon, boy." There were scraping sounds of cutlery against crock, the very briefest of pauses, and then the clatter of a tin plate being driven across the scullery floor by an eager tongue. Pip smiled. Betsy was right about the child and the dog, they were inseparable, and it added greatly to Betsy's peace of mind to know that where Skippy went, Punch would not be far behind. The dog even took sides against his master, as Pip discovered one evening when, in the middle of a mad romp, Sam raised his hand in a playful threat to spank the little girl, and was met by bared teeth and a warning growl from his own dog.

"You'll get rid of him, I suppose?" Stella eyed the romp with distaste. She never stayed after the meal to join in the evening fun as Pip did; she enjoyed the nightly bedtime games, and usually finished up reading Skippy a bedtime story to calm her down enough for sleep.

"Get rid of him? What, Punch?" Sam looked astonished. "Nay, lass, that I'll not. He's doing his job, and we both know it." He dropped his granddaughter on to the floor beside the dog, and rubbed the shaggy head with affection. "Get rid of him? The very idea!" He stumped off, muttering, to his nightly round of locking up, giving Stella a glance in passing that spoke volumes. With Pip he was invariably friendly and at ease, but she noticed that he always avoided Stella if he could, and even Betsy's warmhearted nature tended to become withdrawn when she came in for her meals. Pip glanced across at her colleague, stirring her coffee to make it cool more quickly.

"I'll have to be off soon if Giles has finished his meal. He'll expect me there the moment he's swallowed the last crumb," she guessed drily.

"Keep him waiting." Stella blew a smoke ring lazily, and added more cream to her own cup. "It does men good, now and then."

It wouldn't do her much good if she did, thought Pip, and despatched her drink with far more speed than she had any right to, considering its temperature.

"I'll pop upstairs and get a notebook," she excused herself, and got up. It was no use her waiting for Stella to finish, she would drink her coffee and smoke her long cigarette in a leisurely fashion no matter how long it took. She seemed to use them as a substitute for most meals, thought Pip wonderingly, and realised for the first time that she had never heard Betsy scold Stella for not eating, the same as she scolded Pip, and evidently did the same to Giles. Pip admired her landlady's courage, and wondered why it was that Giles had no appetite. Ever since ... Betsy had said. Ever since what? And why weren't things normal? Obviously Giles had some sort of worry that she, Pip, knew nothing about, but since he didn't confide in his hired staff she wasn't likely to know, she reflected, hoping just the same that it was nothing too serious. That could explain why she had never seen him smile except when he was with the child. His short temper she dismissed as part of his make-up, and then wondered if she was being unjust. She had never heard him speak sharply to Betsy or Sam; he was invariably calm when he was with them.

She shrugged and ran upstairs to get her notebook. A quick flick of her hairbrush through her short curls while she was in her room sufficed to ruffle them into a golden ball about her head, giving her a pixieish look as they curled about her tiny ears, flat against her head, and tinted pink with the warmth of the house after the cold of the morning outside. She didn't look much older than Skippy when she knocked on the door of the drawing room in Giles' quarter of the building, and stuck her head through the opening at his instant "Come in". He sat in a deep wing chair beside a bright log fire, an elegant small table at his elbow holding a tray of coffee things. Pip noticed there were two cups on the tray, and wondered if he was expecting a visitor. She hoped so, it would shorten her own time with him, and set her free more quickly.

"Ah, Pip – come and sit down." He indicated the chair opposite to him, and roused himself in his own, sitting upright and pulling his feet back from the middle of the rug, the alertness returning to his face, but not before Pip had had time to notice the lines of tiredness about his eyes, and the sag to his body as he lay relaxed in his chair, that was never evident in his springy stride while he was about the nursery premises during the day. She hesitated, a swift compunction stirring her for her vexation with him earlier.

"If I'm disturbing you. . . ." she began, backing towards the door, and he raised a quick hand to restrain her.

"You're not, I asked you to come." Once more he waved her to the opposite chair, and this time she sat down on the edge of the seat, her notebook clutched in nervous fingers. He gave her a brief look, and again that swift gleam appeared in his eyes, or it could have been a reflection of the dancing flames that lit the logs in the grate. Without haste he turned to the table, reached for the coffee pot, and poured out two cups. "Betsy provided us with some coffee. I hear you haven't eaten your lunch either," he said surprisingly, handing her the other cup. "Since we've both had a scolding, we might as well console ourselves together," and he smiled.

Pip stared at him. She couldn't help it. It wasn't only the smile, which was practically the first one that had come her way from her employer, even during her interview for the job he had been seriously businesslike, it was the effect it had on his face. He looked years younger, and – and – human! thought Pip, astonished. She took the coffee cup from him with nerveless fingers, and for a second or two he held on to it, patently afraid that she might drop it and the hot contents into her lap.

"Now – this function at the Manor Hotel next month." His crisp tone brought her back to reality, and she grasped the saucer, allowing him to release it with safety. "You already know the hotel," he said, "you've decorated for two functions there already, so you'll know the big ballroom as well as the main entrance. Those will need floral decoration, and there will be the two smaller rooms leading off. The function itself is on the last Saturday in April, so you'll have four clear weeks to sort something out. The proprietor has offered free access to the rooms in the meantime if you want to measure up your available space."

Pip put her cup down on the table, and started to scribble. He evidently didn't intend saying anything about her unfortunate remark to the newspaper reporter, and she relaxed, sure of herself on her own ground, immersed in the detail of her work so that she could forget herself, and to a certain extent her companion, her keen mind seeking information, questioning Giles about times and number of guests, so that she could have some idea how much room would be needed for people, and how much she could commandeer for her decorative effects.

"What is the do in aid of?" she enquired. It always helped to know, because she liked to gear her effects to the particular point of the function itself.

"The local orthopaedic hospital want a therapeutic swimming pool for the children," he answered her quietly. "They're over a thousand pounds short of their target, and we're hoping to make it for them in the one evening."

"It's a good deal of money. . . ." Pip said doubtfully, taken aback by the height of the target.

"Nevertheless, we're banking on it," he responded. "With the summer coming on there won't be much chance for dances and so on to raise more money, and a firm of local contractors have said if the hospital order now they'll do the job at a fixed price. It's too good an opportunity to miss," he finished simply.

"I'll be glad to help," Pip smiled, her sympathy readily aroused. This was something that would have the whole-hearted support of her own family, and she felt suddenly eager not to let Giles Shieldon down. "Have you got any suggestions?" she asked him, "anything special in mind?"

"Nothing, except I want you to remember that the whole thing is for the children," he reminded her. "Oh, there is one thing. I thought the table decorations could be kept fairly simple, so that they could be sent to the hospital afterwards, for the children themselves. It would be nice for them to have some share in the evening, as well as the benefit of their pool later on," he smiled again, showing a softness that Pip would not have suspected of him. Or would she? Having seen him with Skippy, she knew he must be fond of children.

"What's my ceiling cost?" She was briskly business-like. Costing was an inevitable part of her submissions, since each particular assignment had to be quoted for before it was begun, and Pip's job necessarily included an up-to-date awareness of the financial side of her work.

"There's no ceiling on this one." Giles' voice did not encourage questions, but Pip's surprise came through before she could stop herself.

"No ceiling? But you'll want to work out your profit margin before you quote." A sudden suspicion assailed her, coming from she knew not where, except perhaps from the oddly embarrassed look of the man sat opposite to her, and the faint tide of red that crept up under his tan, and that was not due to the warmth of the fire. "You're doing the job for nothing, because it's for the hospital," she accused him. This was an aspect of Giles she hadn't seen before, let alone suspected, and her glance, in his direction, that had before held only wary dislike, now gained a sudden respect.

"Keep this to yourself." His voice was firm, commanding. "It's not generally known, and I don't want it to be."

This was the sort of atmosphere Pip had been brought up in, this quiet giving that shunned publicity, and sought only to alleviate another's need. She warmed to the man's action, readily acquiescent and eager to help. If Giles was doing this, it was probably as much a part of him as it was of her own parents, she reflected. Her guess had been pure intuition, and the fact that he disliked its accuracy was evident in his face.

"I won't talk," Pip assured him quietly. "But I'd like to help all I can," she added, with such obvious sincerity that the man's face softened, and he relaxed in his chair.

"It's a good deal of money to collect," he said soberly, "but we simply must get that pool for them. If it will only help one of them to run around normally, like Skippy does, it will be worth it."

"What about the caterers?" Pip couldn't help asking,

Giles had mentioned a firm of wide repute. "If they're giving the dinner...."

"They're not." Her companion's voice was crisp. "After all, they're not local people," he excused them. "Shieldons is a local firm, and the thing is in the interest of our own district." That wasn't strictly true, the orthopaedic hospital was known far and wide, and took patients in from all over the country, but she let it pass, sympathetic to Giles' withdrawal. "I see I've enlisted your interest in our cause," he sidetracked her questioning.

"I come from a family of doctors," she explained. "But you know that." She'd told him at her interview. "So of course I'm interested in anything like this. Not in causes like environmentalists and their elm trees, though," she added. She didn't know what made her say it, except that Giles hadn't mentioned the matter, and she didn't think she could bear to have it hanging over her head any longer.

"Forget that." His glance was keen, direct. "You weren't to know that the man was a reporter." Evidently it was the nearest he intended to go to an apology for shouting at her, but Pip breathed a sigh of relief, thankful that the subject was in the open, and finished with as far as she was concerned. "I'll see the man himself as soon as I get the opportunity." His voice was grim, and Pip hoped the reporter's shoulders were broad – they would need to be to take the slating he would get, she thought.

"I'll cost the job for you just the same." He would need to know how much capital she was using, for booking purposes. "Can I have a free hand?"

"Absolutely free." His voice was adamant. "Particularly now I've enlisted you on our side." He made no attempt to hide his satisfaction, and Pip wondered whose side he thought she'd been on all the months she'd worked at the nursery. Her loyal spirit rose at the thought of being doubted, but she subdued her feelings, unwilling to risk further dissent.

"I'll make sure you have something special, to give the people who come to the do their money's worth," she promised. He had mentioned the price of the tickets, which made her wince, but according to the quantity he hoped to sell there should be a good profit for the hospital, even taking into account that the hotel had called in a firm of caterers to cope with the dinner, as Pip knew the Manor at Mossly usually did with functions of this size, rather than over-stretch their own facilities, even though these were of the highest order. She gathered up her book with its scribbled notes, and prepared to depart. "Thank you for the coffee." Surprisingly, she found she had enjoyed it. If she'd known when she came in that he was going to share his coffee with her, she would have thought the drink would choke her.

"Pip. . . ." Giles rose from his chair, and checked her as she turned towards the door.

"Yes?" His tone was oddly hesitant, most unlike the Giles she knew, and she wondered what other surprise he had in store.

"Er – I did mention, didn't I, that you'd be expected to stay at the Manor for the evening?" His voice trailed off uncertainly, and Pip's eyebrows rose.

"Yes, you said you wanted me there. I haven't got anything booked for that evening, I kept it free specially." What was bothering him now? she wondered, with a return of her old impatience. He'd told her to be there, and she would be there. That was that, so far as she was concerned.

"I wondered – er – it'll mean evening dress. . . ." Again his voice trailed off, and a spasm of amusement passed through her.

So that was his trouble! He didn't know if she'd got a dress to go in. Perhaps he was afraid she would turn up in working trousers, she thought with an inward gurgle, and disgrace him on the spot.

"I've got something that will do," she assured him,

31

and added wickedly, "If I haven't I can always call on Stella for help."

"Her dresses wouldn't suit you."

His sharp answer turned her round, and with a sigh of resignation she saw the frown on his forehead.

"Back to square one," she thought, her spirits dropping. Oh well, it had been nice while it lasted. Like the unexpected warmth of the sunshine that morning, it had been good to bask for a while, but evidently the frost had returned so far as Giles was concerned. He just have noticed Stella's dresses, though it didn't sound as if he entirely approved, she thought. She didn't herself. Stella's clothes were as exotic as her personality. When she was going out for the evening she frequently wore one of the orchids she grew and as an adornment on Stella it didn't look at all out of place, though Pip had often wondered what would happen if the flower became unclipped – the other girl's taste in evening wear verged on the daring. If such a disaster happened Pip had no doubt Stella would deal with it calmly, her poise seemed unshakeable, but reviewing her own wardrobe she had to acknowledge that the two evening dresses she had brought with her, and which had never been out of their covers since she came to Shieldons, were unsophisticated compared with those her colleague regularly wore. "Oh well. . . ." She shrugged disinterestedly. One of them would do for the evening, she was on duty and would not be expected to be glamorous.

She wondered who Giles would partner. She had seen no evidence that he might be courting; there were few personal visitors to the house, and those who came seemed to be mostly married couples. Several of them Betsy had described to her as "county", and Pip did not doubt that she was correct, for his personal visitors were usually marked by unostentatious quality that clearly indicated their origin, though Pip had always found them unassumingly friendly when they toured the nursery with her employer, and now and then paused to speak to her if she happened to be working nearby. Pip enjoyed talking to them, responding to their genuine interest in her occupation, and invariably found them knowledgeable in the matter of gardens, probably because their houses were usually surrounded by a generous slice of land in which they took an interest. Doubtless they would attend the function as well, though Pip had no fear that the dress she had decided to wear would look out of place among them, she didn't doubt that their evening dress would be as discreetly well chosen as their day wear, and her own dress was a good one.

She slipped it out of its cover in the wardrobe and held it up to the light. It was in a heavy, dull silk, with a high altar neckline that framed her face, the clear leaf green colour richly soft. It was a dress made for dancing, sleeveless and fitting close over the bodice and hips, but below the knees falling into deep pleats that when it was still showed nothing of the vivid colour that backed the folded material. It was only when she was dancing, and the pleats swung wide, that they revealed the rainbow circle of the colour that lined them, each pleat in a different hue, so that the dip and sway of the dance encircled her in a brilliant halo, which when the music ceased to draw her feet along with its rhythm, folded quietly to rest, as the petals of a flower fold together when the evening comes, until the sun coaxes them open again to display their beauty before its warming rays.

"Ooh, fancy! You're going to a ball. A real one!" Skippy had been taken to the pantomime the previous month, and the wonder of Cinderella's magic evening still remained with her. "How lovely, to dance. . . ." She spread her small arms wide, and pirouetted on the rug, where she promptly tripped over Punch, who lay sprawled full length in front of the fire, and landed in an ungainly heap beside the mongrel.

"With my luck, that's about what I should do, trip up

at the crucial moment," laughed Pip. "But I don't expect I shall be dancing," she disabused the small enthusiast, "I'm only going with Mr. Shieldon to look after the flowers. Just to make sure they're happy," she added, with a smile at Skippy's rapt face.

"Who cares about the flowers?" drawled Stella, fitting yet another cigarette into the long amber holder she used, and inhaling with deep, satisfied puffs.

"Come and share my pudding." Hastily Pip distracted Skippy, who had come in to join them earlier tonight for her bedtime story. Pip reached for another chair and tucked her under the table beside her own place, anything to break the child's fascinated stare. Before Stella came she had never seen anyone use a cigarette holder, and her unabashed interest invariably drew an irritated response from its owner.

"I'm going in my green dress, did I show it to you?" Pip relied on Stella's usual interest in clothes to wipe off the disapproving frown which she usually wore when Skippy was in the room.

"Yes, I saw it." Stella's voice was the reverse of enthusiastic. "It's a bit on the plain side, but I suppose if you're only going there to work it won't matter. You could have borrowed one of my old ones, otherwise," she said condescendingly.

"I'm shorter than you," Pip refused hastily, lest Stella press the point. "And fatter," she added craftily, leaning on her companion's pride in her figure, which to Pip's eyes looked frankly thin instead of slender, Stella's habit of taking coffee and cigarettes instead of proper meals giving her a gaunt look that was accentuated by her tallness. "You'd have made a good model," she discovered, "you like nice clothes." She had often wondered what brought Stella into orchid growing. It seemed such an unlikely career for the other girl, who was the type to wear the flowers rather than take the trouble to rear them.

"Orchids offered better prospects at the time," Stella

34

responded drily. "My dear husband was an orchid grower," she added.

"Oh, I see." So that explained it, thought Pip. She knew Stella was separated from her husband; she had let the information slip in a bitter comment one day just after Pip arrived, when the two had been marooned at the nursery for a whole week during the course of a particularly ferocious snowstorm. Pip had contented herself with catching up on reading and letter writing, but Stella had been bored to distraction, and made no attempt to hide the fact that she was bored with the company she found at the nursery, finding it a poor substitute for her usual escorts. All hope of going to her usual haunts for an evening of dancing had been destroyed by blocked lanes, which were impassable for anything but a snow plough from a few yards outside the nursery gates, and she had gathered with Pip and Betsy and her family in the small parlour to watch the television. She seemed to have no resources of her own to keep her interested, and Pip found her casual acceptance of a wrecked marriage more than a little distasteful to her own strictly old-fashioned views of that institution.

"We're quite good friends really, now we're apart," Stella commented casually to the room at large. "We just got bored with one another I suppose, the same as those two," she waved her cigarette holder at the picture on the screen, which portrayed a fictional broken marriage that had sparked off her own earlier comment. "You have to be civilised about these things," she added loftily, and Pip wondered whether uncivilised would have been a better description. From the looks on the faces of Betsy and Sam they shared her views, for to Pip, listening to the solemn beauty of the marriage service as either a bridesmaid or a guest at various of her friends' weddings, the vows taken were real and binding, not to be entered into lightly, and certainly not broken in this casual fashion.

"I wish you were coming to the dinner dance as well." Pip's generous nature instinctively sought to share, even though she did not care for her companion. "I know I'm only going to work, but it will be an outing, and a change." She found herself looking forward to dressing up, it seemed ages since she had been in evening clothes.

"Oh, I don't know. It sounds a bit 'county', as Betsy puts it." Stella's voice held derision. "Those sort of do's can be stuffy, a foxtrot's about the most exciting thing they run to, usually," she said sarcastically. "I'd rather go to a nightclub any time, at least there's a bit more go in their floor shows." She confirmed Pip's earlier guess as to her usual whereabouts when she went out, the hours at which she was wont to arrive back at her flat pointed to her choice of amusement during her free time.

"There might be some interesting people there. Some of Giles' friends seem nice." All the ones she had met she liked, reflected Pip, and if they came to the function it would mean that she would know a few people there at least.

"Giles' friends?" Stella's lip curled. "You can keep them for me," she sneered derisively. "From what I've seen of them around here they're not my cup of tea. Of course, there's Giles himself," she murmured provocatively. "It might be interesting to see if he can be roused." She met Pip's shocked glance with a mocking look, ignoring her warning nod towards the child. "If he's capable of being roused, that is," there was a calculating gleam in her eye that reminded Pip of a hunting cat. "But as I said, it might be an interesting pastime to find out."

"Come and help me to decide what flowers to use for the function." Pip drew Skippy on to her lap, unwilling to let the conversation continue its present trend in front of the child, and aware that, her pudding finished, she was taking an unwelcome interest in what Stella was saying. "What are your favourite flowers?"

"Daisies," Skippy's reply was prompt and decided. "In a long chain," she spread her arms wide, reminding Pip of her earlier attempt to dance.

"Daisy chains – that's it!" Pip sketched swiftly, intent on her task, her pencil busily trying to keep pace with her ideas.

"You're not working now, surely?" Stella sounded amazed. "Don't say Himself has scared you into working in the evenings," she jibed.

"Of course not." Pip flushed, unwilling to appear priggish. "But I'm interested. Giles has given me a free hand, no expense spared." She didn't break her confidence and tell Stella that their employer was bearing the brunt of the cost himself. "Besides, it's for the hospital, so I don't mind," she added, trying hard not to let her annoyance show.

"I'll leave you to get on with it. I'm going to wash my hair." Stella flounced out, back to her flat. She never stayed long after the meal, usually she had gone out by now, and Pip wondered if for once her latest boy-friend had let her down. She dropped a quick kiss on Skippy's small face as Betsy came in and claimed the protesting youngster for bed.

"We'll leave you in peace," her landlady promised, and Pip smilingly shook her head.

"Skippy's just given me a great idea for a big function," she told her. "I was stuck until she helped me out," she lied, smiling at the quick flush of pleasure that made the cheeks of the six-year-old rosy under her freckles.

"I helped her, Gran, I reely did," her clear little voice piped back through the closing door, and Pip mentally tied another knot in her hanky to add to the one for the Easter egg the moment she reached the shops. Skippy had helped her, more than she knew, and she would make sure she didn't go unrewarded. "Remember the whole thing is to benefit the children," Giles had said. His casual remark had stayed in her mind, and Skippy capped it. Children and daisy chains were synonymous, the tiny white flowers the very essence of innocent childhood. The sight of Skippy twirling, arms outstretched, across the rug, came back to tug at her mind, the joyous grace of impulsive movement stirring her imagination. Not the tumble at the end, of course, that was pure Skippy, so engrossed in her dance that she didn't notice Punch lay across the rug. The thought of the auburn-haired sprite fluttering across the floor, light as a zephyr, and lost in a world of her own imagination, stilled Pip's pencil.

"If it will only help one of them to run around normally, like Skippy does. . . ." Again Giles' words came back to her, replacing her mental vision of free-limbed grace with the halting squeak of crutches that had become so familiar to her while she was at home, and often used her spare time to help out in the wards of the local hospital where her parents were both consultants. Her face sobered, and she thoughtfully stroked in the petals of another daisy. "Single chrysanths will do, they're the nearest thing to daisies, they'll be the right size to show up, and tough enough to stand up to the job," she decided. She knew that Giles had a good selection of forced ones in the greenhouses. "Thank goodness we can get chrysanths throughout the year," the thought was a relief. "Yellow ones would do nicely, they show up well, and represent sunshine." That, too, went with children. Her pencil speeded up, but she let her thoughts wander. Often an idea would come if it was allowed to develop on its own. She had seen chrysanthemum heads fresh after several days when they were used to make a living collage for a well-dressing ceremony she had the good fortune to come across while she was on holiday one year. A picture in flowers. Again, a vision of the dancing child flitted across her mind and she began to sketch, letting her pencil roam where it would.

"My, but that's pretty! You do draw well, Miss Pip."
Pip looked up from her work, dazed with concentration,
to find Betsy beside her with a hot milk drink and a plate
of biscuits. "It's supper time, lovie. And high time you
had a rest," she scolded gently. "You've been at work all
the evening." She put down her offering and took the
sketch block from Pip's lap. "That's real nice. It looks a
bit like our Skippy," she discovered.

"She gave me the whole idea," Pip acknowledged,
stretching arms that she hadn't realised until now were
cramped. "Ooh, I'm stiff! I didn't notice the time go
by," she confessed, eyeing her evening's work critically.
"It shows up better when you hold it away," she
acknowledged, tilting her head on one side the better to
view the sketch that her landlady held so that the lamplight fell on it, highlighting the figures of two children,
a boy and a girl, dancing across a carpet of flowers, their
small faces alight with laughter, and a daisy chain linking
their uplifted hands.

"I've done it vaguely with the idea of filling in the
front of the orchestra dais in the hotel ballroom – there's
a fairly generous space there that's never used for dancing." Pip's memory of the Manor Hotel served her well.
"We could perhaps link the fittings round the walls with
daisy chains. And then there's the room being used for
the dinner, we'd want something special in that, too."
Her gaze became abstracted, her hand holding the glass
of hot beverage stilled in mid-air as her mind wandered.
"Then there's the table decorations. I don't know where
Giles will sit. . . ."

"In his usual place, I expect," said Betsy briskly, returning the sketch to her lap. "And if you don't look
careful, you'll have your drink all over the tray," she
warned her. "The place for your supper is inside you, not
spilled everywhere," she brought Pip back to earth. "You
had next to nothing for your lunch."

39

"I had a good dinner this evening," protested Pip, defending her treatment of Betsy's good cooking. After anyone had taken so much trouble to produce a meal, she could understand it causing offence if it was rejected.

"Well, that's one of you with your appetite back, anyway," Betsy allowed grudgingly. So that meant Giles hadn't eaten his dinner, either. Pip wondered what could be worrying him. At all events she could make sure the details for the function were not the cause. She determined to do her level best to make sure nothing went wrong with this particular commission. Nothing did go wrong with her jobs normally, she was too meticulous about detail to allow for mistakes, but this was evidently something that was very close to her employer's heart.

"I'll put it away for tonight, and think about it again in the morning," she promised, tackling her supper with an energy that brought an approving nod from her landlady. "I'll have to get it all down on paper, and then find out if Mr. Shieldon approves before I can do anything concrete about it." Giles had given her a free hand, but that didn't mean to say he wouldn't want to know what she had in mind before she set the wheels in motion to carry out her paper suggestions.

"I'll have to get Giles' approval," she reminded herself sleepily later, snuggling under the warm eiderdown, her mind still running on Skippy and the daisy chains. Somehow she found herself holding one up for Giles to see, and her dreaming mind waited for his smile, but none came. He never seemed to smile. Suddenly the daisy chain turned into one of Stella's dresses. "She said I could borrow it," she told him, but he didn't seem to hear, and the frown on his face blackened as she had seen it do so often since she came to work for him, and then it changed quickly, unexpectedly, into a smile. The sort of smile he had given her when she went to see him after lunch, and he nodded approvingly, and she found that Stella's dress had turned into her own green dance frock with the coloured lining to the pleats, that floated rainbow bright about her feet as he took her in his arms and swung her into a dance on a floor that was a carpet of flowers.

CHAPTER THREE

"I'M going to wander round the greenhouses to see if I can get some ideas." Pip stuck her head into the kitchen after breakfast the next morning to let Betsy know where she could find her if she was wanted. Giles was stood in the opening of the outside door, and she nodded good morning, and pulled the hall door to hurriedly to stop the draught. Quickly she slipped her blue woolly over her head, grabbed her sketch book and pencil and mentally sorted out her route so that she should not waste time walking backwards and forwards unnecessarily. She hadn't a lot of work in the way of orders today, and those that she had could quite well be done by the girl she was training as her assistant. It would be good experience for her, and leave Pip free to work on her ideas for the coming function. The polo neck of her woolly ruffled her springy curls, but she didn't bother to go up to her room again to comb them; the brisk wind outside would soon undo any work she put into them, she decided. It was blowing hard, in rough blustery gusts that seemed to be getting stronger.

"They say if March comes in like a lamb it goes out like a lion," said Sam, reversing the old saw, "and I reckon we'll end the month with a real good blow," he predicted with gloomy relish the night before, as a particularly hard puff hit the cottage chimney, and mischievously sent the smoke from their log fire back into the room.

"There now, something will happen, you see," prophesied Betsy, wiping her streaming eyes. To Pip it seemed more reasonable to suppose that the chimney needed a good sweep and a cowl on the top, but to her superstitious landlady it was an omen of the darkest portent, and Pip met Sam's wink with a face that tried not to smile.

"Well, maybe it'll be something nice," she comforted, and wondered as she stepped out into the bright sunshine towards the greenhouses what it might be.

"I'm getting as bad as Betsy!" she exclaimed, deriding herself for being superstitious.

"And what's wrong with Betsy?" an enquiring voice asked above her head. A dark shadow fell across the gravelled path in front of her, and Giles' feet crunched on the surface at a speed designed to catch her up. "Oh, she's expecting something awful to happen." Pip smiled. "The smoke blew down the chimney last night and. . . ."

"And Betsy believes in old wives' tales. I know," Giles nodded understanding. "I'll have the thing swept, and a cowl fixed on the top," he promised gravely, and Pip's lips curved upwards. She looked up and met the twinkle in his eyes, and let her amusement show through.

"It might save her a few sleepless nights," she agreed laughingly, "though there's not much you can do about the smoke that's already come down."

"Maybe we can make something nice happen, just to convince her," Giles smiled back. "I heard you say you were going round the greenhouses. I'll come along with you, perhaps we can pool our ideas. Betsy said you already had something sketched out?"

"Yes, Skippy gave me the idea really." Pip was nothing if not honest. "I'll get her a toffee bar the next time I'm in the village, she deserves something for the inspiration." She paused, hesitating. "Would you like to see what I've sketched out so far?" It was a good thing she had brought her block along with her, she thought. Giles could either give her the go-ahead or knock the whole idea on the head before she had put too much work into it.

"Let's go inside out of the wind." He reached out and opened the door of the greenhouse nearest to them. "We can put your notes on the bench and have a look at them in comfort." He shut the door to carefully behind him and leaned down with his elbows comfortably on the bench, his woolly sweater companionably rubbing shoulders with her own. Pip could stand upright, but Giles had to bend his tall frame to bring himself down to her level.

"It's only an idea, really." She flicked open her sketch-block hesitantly, suddenly unsure of herself. Had it been a good idea? Giles had said to remember the whole thing was to benefit the children, but did her sketch look childish? After all, the function itself was going to be attended by grown-ups, and most probably grown-ups with sophisticated tastes. The price of the tickets alone would ensure that those who came would be well-to-do. "So far I've only drafted out a few suggestions for the dinner tables. You said you wanted the decorations there to go to the children at the hospital. I thought maybe those oblong tubs of large flowering pansies and violas, and the pots of miniature roses," she suggested. "They'll keep on flowering for some time, and children like to watch the buds come out." She stole a glance at his face. It gave no indication of his thoughts. One long brown finger ran down her list of possible flowers, and Pip noticed the well manicured nail. Giles Shieldon always looked impeccably groomed. "As I said, they're only ideas, they can easily be scrapped." A wave of depression hit Pip, born of his uncommunicating silence, and suddenly her ideas of the evening before, that she had thought such good ones then, now seemed naïve and rather silly. She would stick to the usual run-of-the-mill decorations, she decided, she could always achieve something with them that carried the stamp of originality which marked all her work.

"This is an inspiration." Giles turned to her, one elbow

still on the bench, so that his face was on a level with her own, and his brown eyes glowed with enthusiasm. "You must have stayed up half the night to work this out, even so far as you've gone."

"It was a bit late when I packed up," Pip admitted, surprised back into good spirits by the force of his approval, and his obvious pleasure in what she had done. "But I haven't really got very far, it's only in outline. There's all the detail to be filled in yet." It meant an immense amount of mental work before the actual physical taking shape of the arrangements could begin, and by the very nature of the material she was using that would not be until the last possible moment, to ensure that the flowers were fresh on the night. She would not have any free hours during the week before the function, so it was as well she did not go out very often, like Stella, she thought drily. "I thought I'd wander round the greenhouses to see what is likely to be available next month, and let a few ideas sink in," she explained her apparently aimless errand; she did not want him to accuse her of wasting time again.

"I'll wander with you." His tone left her in no doubt that he liked her ideas, and was keen to be involved as well.

"I've managed to rouse him, not Stella," thought Pip amusedly, though in a different way from what the other girl had meant, of course.

"What are you smiling at?" His fingers were on her arm, guiding her round some seedboxes that stood ready to receive the young, pricked-out plants, and effectively blocked half the gangway.

"Have these moved, will you, George?" He spoke to the senior foreman who came towards them from the other end of the greenhouse.

"I was just going to, gaffer," the man replied, throwing a frown at the boxes. "I don't like the doorways blocked, you know that."

Giles was careful of the safety of his employees, thought Pip approvingly. She had had such training instilled into her during her years with Grenvilles, so that it was more instinct than anything else now. She was glad of the diversion, for Giles' question was one she wouldn't be able to answer even if she wanted to, and she felt her cheeks burn at the thought of what would happen if he insisted on the reason for her smile. She felt the foreman's eyes on her flushed face, and quickly pushed up the sleeves of her sweater.

"It's hot in here after the wind outside," she hurried on, hoping her excuse was effective, though there wasn't much she could do about it, she reflected, thankfully stepping down from the greenhouse into the long wooden shed that held two rows of workbenches, one on each side, each high stool occupied by a woman busily pricking out bedding plants ready for the spring rush that would come at about the same time as the function she was preparing for, when the winter borders would be cleared of their wallflowers and bulbs, and people would look for plants to provide colour during the summer months ahead.

"You've got a lot of patience," she smiled at the woman nearest to her, whose skilled hands never ceased their planting and firming as she looked up and answered.

"I've got five young 'uns to feed, miss. It gives you a lot of patience," she said significantly, returning to her lobelia seedlings, that of all plants must be the most tedious to handle.

She had a point, conceded Pip, but she hoped nevertheless that the woman enjoyed her work too. It must be awful to work just for money, she thought. She knew the staff were well paid at Shieldons, and knew, too, though not from Giles, that they were allowed so many boxes of plants each when the different seasons came round. Betsy had told her what a glorious sight the village gardens were during the summer months, thanks to Giles' generosity, and the glow of bulbs, and the massed, though still green wallflower plants that she had seen herself while passing through the small community were evidence of an open-handedness that must have brought a lot of pleasure to the villagers, as well as to chance visitors who happened to wander that way.

"Some of the earlier pansies are just starting to show colour in the next house. Come through and see." Giles strode to her side, cheerfully answering the pleasant greetings he received from the women on the way. He was popular with his staff, the men as well as the women respecting his high standards and fairness in rewarding their efforts. "They'll just about be ready when you want them, those at the end, I mean." He pointed to some oblong tubs of healthy-looking green that as yet showed none of the colour of those on the bench nearer to them. "They're bright, and they'll keep on blooming." Giles put out his forefinger and turned the face of the nearest pansy towards them, its deep purple and yellow glowing like rich velvet in the bright sunshine coming through the glass.

"They're lovely." Pip liked pansies too, their cheerful, homely little faces striking a chord within her that the more exotic flowers – like orchids, she thought – could never do. She bent her face down to smell the sweetness of the petals, and passed on slowly, lingering for yet another glance before Giles closed the door behind them and guided her across the wide gravel path towards the next greenhouse on her list. As they emerged into the open air the sound of a concrete mixer hit them with full force, the mechanical rattle-crash so wildly out of place that Pip had not got used to it even yet.

"Sam's happy." Giles sounded amused.

"He'll reckon the day well spent when he gets in to his dinner tonight," agreed Pip. This was another aspect of Giles that she had only just discovered, and which she had at first thought oddly out of character, but since he had spoken to her about providing the flowers for the function she wasn't so sure. The man beside her had a depth that she had not given him credit for, she decided. Betsy had told her about the concrete mixer.

"Sam's that stubborn," she spoke mildly, accepting her husband's odd ways. "He will mix all the potting soil by hand."

"Grenvilles used to buy theirs in," Pip returned, surprised that a nursery of the size of Shieldons didn't do the same. The proprietary brands were expensive, but so was time and labour; the two about balanced one another.

"That's what Mr. Giles wanted to do, but Sam, he was dead set against it," Betsy shook her head. "But the shovelling and carrying, and all that mixing – well, it got too much for him, though he wouldn't give in. You know Sam," she sighed. "That's when Mr. Giles bought him that concrete mixer. He puts his own quantities in, and the machine mixes it for him."

It certainly took all the hard labour out of the operation, and still left Sam with an expert's pride in his own special "mix", which was a secret he guarded closely, and there was no doubt that the results were highly successful – the thriving plants that the nursery produced were sufficient evidence to convince anyone of that. Underneath his stern exterior, Giles had an unexpected softness, Pip discovered. She liked a strength that would unbend to salvage an elderly man's pride, and her heart warmed to his action, though she wouldn't have dared let him know she was aware of what he had done. His reaction when she guessed he would not charge for the flowers for the function told her plainly enough that he didn't like such matters discussed, and it would only get Betsy into trouble if she mentioned it.

Sam raised his hand in silent greeting as they passed towards the greenhouse door, and both Pip and Giles responded in kind. It was useless to shout, the noise would have drowned their voices, and Pip made a smile do. It broadened as she met Sam's delighted grin, her eyes taking in the separate mounds of soil, peat, sand and small gravel piled neatly beside the revolving machine, which made up the ingredients of his various mixes.

"You've got to know the necessary incantations, as well," Giles murmured, accurately guessing her thoughts as he shut the tightly fitting door behind them, cutting off the noise. Pip chuckled.

"Sam's proud of his expertise," she acknowledged, "and I don't wonder," she added loyally, "he seems to get excellent results." The display on the benches in front of them was proof enough, she thought, unable to resist a small gasp of delight that this particular part of the nursery never failed to draw from her.

"You like roses, too." It was a statement rather than a question, and Pip nodded.

"Mmm, I like all the flowers, of course, but roses – well, they're special." Not necessarily the cultivated ones. The wild dog-roses that tangled the hedges lining the lanes of her native village had the same fascination for Pip, the deep, glowing colour in the heart of each tightly furled bud holding as much joy for her as the most exotic, long-stemmed beauty the nursery could produce. Those by which they were surrounded now were miniature varieties, the delicate perfection of every tiny bush bejewelled with colour, each bloom no bigger than her own fingernail.

"They're exquisite!" She made no attempt to hide her appreciation. The glory of the flowers that were the basic materials of her daily work was a living wonder within her that never faded, even though the flowers themselves did, the beauty of texture and colour a perfection that mortal hands, for all their skills, could only imitate, and never form, the elemental creation of life a gift denied the human mind's eternal seeking, its secret withheld, and the awe of wonder for all beauty bestowed instead.

"Tubs of miniature roses, and pansies, for the dinner tables," Pip decided. "That is, if it's all right with you?" she added hastily, remembering in time that Giles was paying for the whole thing. "They'll be more expensive than cut blooms," she stopped doubtfully.

"But more suitable to give to the children in hospital afterwards," Giles put in. "A real live rose bush of their own would please any child," he guessed, "and when I said you'd got a free hand, I meant it," he reminded her, and Pip relaxed.

"That's the material for the tables coped with, then." She descended to practicalities. "I thought, low, ellipse-shaped blocks of colour on the tables, rather than a multi-coloured mixture. Maybe violas, instead of pansies," she murmured thoughtfully, half to herself, sucking the end of her pencil, her mind far away. "I don't like high flowers for table decorations," she wrinkled her nose in a characteristic gesture of disapproval. "You either have to shout round them, or stand on your chair to see over them."

"It must be difficult when you're only five feet and a bit," Giles retorted teasingly, and Pip looked up at him quickly, a spark of spirit showing in her eyes. Her height, or the lack of it, had been a sore point with her since she was capable of being tormented about it by a callous brother, and her expression showed it.

"And don't suck your pencil." A hard brown hand closed round her own and removed the red-painted length of wood from her mouth. "You'll get splinters in your tongue." His tone of voice was the same as he used when he was talking to Skippy, and he grinned down at her, a glint of pure mischief lighting his eyes and showing his teeth in a white gleam against the dark tan of his face. "Use it on this, where it belongs." He flattened the pencil on to her sketch block. "You'll find it more profit-

able. Coming, George!" He waved a hand to his foreman, acknowledging his call from the doorway, and
strode away, leaving Pip fuming beside the rose trees on
the bench, and resisting an urge to pick up one of the
small pots and hurl it and its contents at the back of his
retreating head.

"Go on, throw it!"

A cool, damp plant pot was thrust into Pip's hand, and
Stella's voice, lazily amused, turned her startled glance
over her shoulder. She hadn't heard her colleague approach along the duckboard walk in between the rows of
benches, and looked down without thinking.

"I've got sneakers on." Stella held up one foot, encased in a far from white tennis shoe. For someone with
such exotic looks, thought Pip, and a love of glamorous
evening clothes, her working attire was often surprisingly
scruffy. I suppose she doesn't need to bother, with her
looks, she mused, regarding her companion's dark-
haired beauty. She would look lovely in a sack, she decided, doubts about the suitability of her own evening
dress beginning to trouble her. Not that she could do
anything about it now. The Easter holiday was next
weekend, and there'd be no time for shopping afterwards; there would be too much to do if she was to perfect her plans on time.

"You don't usually come through the greenhouses."
She returned to her companion's unexpected presence
on this side of the nursery. Stella normally kept exclusiv-
ely to her own orchid house, not deigning to take the
trouble to make friends with the rest of the nursery staff,
with whom Pip had quickly been on speaking terms from
the first week she arrived. "Did you want some pot plants
for something?" She indicated the glow of colour beside
them.

"No, I took a short cut to get out of the wind," Stella
shrugged away the roses with barely a glance. "It's blowing a gale outside." She tossed her long mane of hair

back from her face, where the wind had fingered it into a jet tangle about her head and shoulders. "And I saw you in here with Giles," she smiled slyly, "so I thought I'd come in and see what was going on."

"There's nothing going on." Pip's face radiated honest astonishment, and the lurking gleam in the other girl's dark eyes brightened.

"D'you know, I believe you," she laughed. "With anyone else, now – myself, for instance. . . ." She stopped significantly.

"What on earth could go on in the middle of a greenhouse?" A helpless chuckle shook Pip. "I can't imagine a more public place, surrounded by all that glass," she laughed. Nor a less likely companion than Giles, she thought, although she didn't say so out loud. Apart from the fact that he was her employer, which didn't seem to bother Stella in the least, all men seemed to be lumped into one category with her. Giles' manner invariably held a stern reserve that Pip found slightly repelling, despite the new respect she had discovered for him during the last few days. She didn't know which she liked less, Giles criticising her, or Giles laughing at her. His condescending tone still rankled from when he had taken her pencil from her, and the knowledge that her annoyance had shown, and had amused him, did not make her feel any calmer.

"I'll walk back with you." She shrugged her thoughts away from her. It was no use glowering, she decided, her sense of humour coming to her rescue; she would need all her energies for concentrating on the job she had in hand. Reluctantly she left the crowded rose bushes behind. If she had been on her own she would have lingered for a while to enjoy them, but conscious of Stella's boredom with anything but her own particular sphere of work she followed the other girl out of the door, and gasped as the wind caught at her, taking her breath and her balance with a terrific gust that left her staggering in the quick calm that followed it.

"It wouldn't be so bad if it blew steadily," Stella put out a hand to keep herself on her feet, "it's these intermittent whoofs that catch you unawares." She slammed the greenhouse door shut.

"Skippy's having trouble keeping her feet." Pip saw the child and the dog racing along the gravel path in the direction that Giles and the foreman had taken earlier. The gust stopped her in mid-scamper, and for a hectic moment she and the dog found themselves in an unresisting tangle, then the gust passed and they sorted themselves out and ran on.

"I expect she's looking for George, he keeps a pocket full of sweets," Pip smiled, aware that it was not only Giles who spoiled the child. The foreman seemed equally fond of her, and she was often to be seen riding his shoulder, with Punch trotting faithfully behind.

"I expect he'd rather give his sweets to Skippy's mum," Stella commented observantly. "Now there's something really going on," she jibed, deliberately trying to bring the colour to Pip's cheeks.

"What, Skippy's mother and George? Oh, I hope you're right!" Pip turned eager eyes to her companion. "Skippy likes him, it's obvious. Not only for the sweets," she added. "George is nice. I've often wondered why he wasn't married." The foreman would be about in his early thirties, she guessed, and she knew he was a single man; he lodged in the village with one of the other nursery workers and his wife. "Skippy's mother has been on her own for a long time. Betsy told me Skippy was only just one when her father died. It couldn't have been easy for her mother, bringing up a baby single-handed," she said sympathetically. "It's a good job she has Betsy and Sam."

"Unless my guess is way out, she'll soon have George as well," Stella commented drily, "and I don't think my guess is wrong."

"You're more observant than me, at least about that sort of thing." Pip acknowledged that she tended to take things – and people – at their face value. "I like happy endings," she sighed, her generous heart, that had so far remained whole except for one or two teenage crushes, devastating while they lasted, but transient, warming to the happy solution that the future seemed to hold in store for three people whom she liked.

"They're the exception rather than the rule." Stella screwed up her face in a wry grimace.

"Oh, Stella, I'm sorry! I should have thought. . . ." Instantly contrite, Pip turned to the other girl. "I forgot you – your. . . ."

"My dear husband and I split up? Don't let it worry you," her companion sneered. "It doesn't bother me, so why should you be concerned?"

Did it bother Stella? Pip had often wondered about that, too. There was a hard note to the other girl's laughter when she mentioned her husband that hinted of bitterness, and it was an undoubted fact that she chain-smoked incessantly, with a restless, nervous energy that might be a part of her make-up, but might also be an aftermath of her broken marriage. It would be nice if Stella could get married again, thought Pip. But she wasn't divorced yet, only separated, so that wouldn't be possible until she got a decree, with all the formalities that had to be gone through first. Pip shuddered inwardly at the cold, impersonal destruction of something so precious, that had started out so full of hope and happiness.

"Come on." Stella threw down her cigarette, and ground the butt into lifelessness on the gravel beneath her heel. "If we follow Giles and George we can cut through the last of the greenhouses and get back indoors that way. Are you going to your workroom?"

"No, I want to finish some sketches, I've got a girl coping with the routine orders," Pip shouted back, raising her voice to make herself heard above the wind. "If

54

we were out on the common with a kite, this would be fun." She would have to make the suggestion to Skippy, with Easter ahead she would have some free time during the holiday, and if the wind kept blowing like this it would make ideal kite weather. She didn't know what Stella was doing for Easter, she hadn't asked her, but she doubted if the other girl would join such an expedition. On her off duty days she usually remained in bed until about lunch time, and never seemed to come alive until she was ready to go dancing in the evening, which wasn't much good when you were going kite flying, Pip decided.

She loved the common land that lay on the other side of the village, a huge, open area of gorse and ling that, from its lack of four-footed population, seemed unsuitable even for grazing, but made an ideal spot to walk and blow away the cobwebs of the week before the routine of work closed in again. Pip spent most Sunday afternoons there; she jokingly said it helped to work off Betsy's good lunch, but in fact she loved the solitude, finding in the quiet, lonely hours of walking a refreshment of the spirit that was more to her than physical rest. Pip liked her fellow human beings, but an hour or two away from them now and then, on the rough heathland, exchanging their company for the wild inhabitants she met along the solitary tracks, brought her busy life into its proper perspective, and if anything served to increase her enjoyment of it.

"You can keep your kite flying, all I want to do is to get indoors and get my breath back. Look, there's Giles and George making for the greenhouse now, if we hurry we can catch them up." Stella quickened her pace, and Pip had to break into a trot to keep up with her long-legged stride. She would have preferred to follow Giles at her own pace – one not destined to catch him up. She didn't mind the airy buffetings, finding them preferable to the criticism that she so often sensed from her employer, but the wind didn't tangle her hair into her eyes as it did with Stella's long mane, which served to make her irritable. Pip wondered why she didn't rubber-band it into a ponytail during the day; it would have been out of her way during working hours, even if it might not have looked so glamorous.

"Skippy's seen them, too. She's turning back." Pip watched as the child started to return along the gravel path, running easily now with the wind at her back. It ruffled Punch's hair until it stood up around the little mongrel, making him look like some prehistoric creature about to attack, which was maligning the little fellow, thought Pip with a smile. He was cheerfully friendly with everyone so long as they didn't threaten his young charge.

"Heavens, look how that elm tree's bending!" Stella paused in her headlong rush towards the greenhouse door. "If it goes on like this it'll...."

"Skippy! Run!"

Pip's feet took wings at the same time as her shout. The elm tree leaned over, straining to withstand the wind, but age and brittleness, and a huge head of branches, made it an impossible task, and with a groan that was near human the roots on the upwind side gave way to a force that was greater than their strength, and released the huge stem, whose enormous height curved with rapidly increasing speed towards the end of the long greenhouse, and the figures of the running child and the dog.

Pip's heart was a fierce pain in her side, her breath coming in great gasps. She would never reach Skippy in time, the child would be engulfed, her small legs were incapable of beating the speed of the tree. And then she saw another figure dart from the shelter of the greenhouse door. A second followed it, and Giles and then George were both running as well, running towards Skippy whose small arms were stretched out to catch at them, terror pressing her legs to run to the limit of their six-year-old strength. Pip wanted to press her hands to her eyes, not daring to look, and yet not daring to look away, and then the lower branches of the tree hit the end of the greenhouse. The glass exploded with a sharp bang, loud enough to momentarily drown the sound of the wind, and for a few brief, vital seconds the structure of the greenhouse held the weight of the tree, delaying its fall, giving Giles time to grab Skippy's outstretched hands and pull her into his arms, and then turn and race the other way, clasping the small figure to him and running half bent to protect her at all costs in case his speed should not be enough. With a grinding crack the struts of the greenhouse gave way, and with an earth-shaking thud the elm reached the ground, the tips of its branches only inches away from Giles' running feet.

"Giles! Oh, Giles!"

Surely it was Skippy she was terrified for, before Giles? Pip didn't stop to argue with her own thoughts, she ran on, cannoned into George, running too. They steadied one another and reached Giles and the child. Numbly Pip reached out, and the man relinquished his hold on the little girl, gentling her into Pip's arms, instinctively acknowledging a small child's need of a woman's comfort.

"There, there, it's all right now." Pip patted her gently, soothing her fright, talking away the gasping sobs that were half fear, half lack of breath, until the child's convulsive shivering ceased and she drew a deep breath.

"Punch?"

Her voice was fraught with fear, and she kept her head buried in Pip's shoulder, afraid to look.

"Punch is fine, he wants to come up and see you." Two large, hairy paws threatened her balance, and she felt one of the men gently pull the dog away. Restrained from going to the child, it whined sharply, a high, thin plaint that cut through Skippy's horror and brought her face up from Pip's shoulder. "Stand down and let him see you're all right, that's a good girl. I can't have you both in my arms, I'm not big enough," Pip teased normality back into the child's face, and the dog completed the process, planting two proprietorial paws on her shoulders and running a rough tongue across her cheeks, bringing quick colour into them to replace the ashen fear that had so lately rested there.

"Get down, Punch. Stop it! I've had a wash. . . ." Skippy's belief that washes were an unnecessary waste of time meant a daily tussle with her grandmother, and the dog inflicting an extra one seemed to her to be the last straw. She pushed him down firmly, but held on to his tangle of hair. "He's not hurt, is he, Uncle George?"

"No, love, the tree missed him. So did the glass." Gently the tall foreman bent and folded her into the circle of his arms, and she rested there contentedly, Punch happy to remain at his feet now that he was sure she was whole. "The glass didn't miss you, though, gaffer." There was instant concern in the man's voice as Giles turned round and put up a hand to a red, dripping weal across his one cheek.

"It's nothing."

"Let me see. Sit down on the step." Pip forgot her awe of him, seeing merely the livid cut and the whiteness of his face that had paled his tan to a muddy yellow. "Get me one of the first-aid kits out of the greenhouses, will you, please, George?" There was a comprehensive kit kept in each of the greenhouses and sheds, a thorough precaution of which Pip heartily approved, and blessed the thoughtfulness of the owner for providing it, though he could hardly have expected to use it on himself, she thought, reaching for the opened box which George thrust into her hands.

"It was lucky the tree hit the other end of the house, this side's intact, and the box was just inside the door." George helped her to sort out what she needed, standing by while she damped some cotton wool and quickly swabbed the wound.

"It isn't too deep, I'll put a couple of plaster stitches on and it'll keep the edges closed until you can get proper medical attention." Her voice was brisk, impersonal, responding to the first aid training that her parents had insisted she learned, and glad of it, not for the first time, though as she worked she was conscious of a flutter in her stomach that was not normally there in times of crisis. It's fright, she decided; it was the sight of the elm tree chasing Skippy. She kept her thoughts to herself, unwilling to upset the child further, but she need not have worried. With the quick resilience of the very young, the little girl wriggled out of the circle of the foreman's arm and bent serious eyes on what Pip was doing.

"I runned faster than the tree," she informed her companions proudly. "Does it hurt much? You'll have a bandage." There was a note of envy in her voice, and Giles smiled, and then winced.

"It only hurts when I laugh," he gave the classic reply, and a quick grin enlivened Skippy's face. "Will you do something for me?" The red curls gave a vigorous nod. "Run and tell your gran you're all right, she's bound to be worried." Despite his own fright and injury he was still thoughtful of Betsy's feelings, but as the child ran off, important with her message, Pip felt his body sag back against the struts of the greenhouse. Her concern must have shown in her face, for he instantly pressed himself upright and made to regain his feet. His first attempt was unsuccessful, and Pip knelt beside him, sliding her arm behind his back.

"Link your hands with mine, George, behind his back," she commanded quietly. The foreman gave her a look of surprise, probably at her authoritative tone, which sat oddly on the Pip he was accustomed to, but he did as he was told without question. Would that there were more people like him, thought Pip fervently. The emergency services wouldn't find life half so difficult if there were. "Now, link your arms about our shoulders," she instructed Giles, "and stand up with us." She and George were both crouched on his level, and at her nod the foreman rose to his feet and Pip did the same, bringing Giles up with them, and steadying him until they were sure he was capable of standing on his own.

"Thanks, I'm all right now. I think I'll go inside and clean the blood off, then we can come back and see to this. Make sure no one goes near it, will you, George, in case the rest collapses? We don't want anyone hurt." The foreman nodded, and Giles gingerly tried an experimental step or two away from them. "Don't worry, I'm mobile now," he smiled down at Pip, who had kept pace with him just in case.

"Just the same, I'll help you inside." Stella stepped forward and put her arm protectively about his waist. "Pip's too short for you to lean on, you'd have a list to one side," she smiled at her employer. "Put your arm about my waist." She pulled his hand into place and enclosed her own about it, so that he had no option but to leave it where it was. "Now I'll see you inside, and get you a nice cup of tea."

It was so unlike Stella to feel concern for anyone but herself that Pip could only stare as she walked away with Giles beside her. She couldn't see the man's face, but he didn't seem at all reluctant to go, though the expression in the foreman's eyes was enigmatic as they followed the couple along the gravel path.

"You come a safe distance away too, Miss Pip," he bade her, steering her firmly in the wake of the others, and Pip kept pace with him silently, aware that she trembled, aware of a swift lowering of spirits within her that brought her former cheerfulness to zero. The aftermath of shock, she told herself; it would pass off in good time.

"I think I'll go in for a cup of tea too. Why not join us, George, after you've made sure the staff stay away from the area?" she suggested. "It's been as much a shock for you as it has for us."

"That I will, miss, and glad to," the man retorted fervently. "If them environmentalist folks hadn't interfered in the first place this would never have happened," he added savagely. "Sent their so-called experts, they did, to say the tree was safe. Gaffer said 'twasn't, he was all set to have it felled. And he was right, too." He indicated the trunk, clearly hollow from where the base had slewed round as it fell. "It's a pity they don't turn their minds to something more important, like that road they're agoin' to build," he fumed. "They could do some real good there if they wanted to, 'stead of wasting their time messing about with things like trees."

"Why, what about the road?" Pip kept him talking, easing his shock as it eased hers to listen. "I know there's going to be a bypass built round here, I've heard it talked about in the nursery."

"An' have you heard where it's supposed to be agoin'?" The foreman glared in her direction.

"Well, no . . . across the common, I supposed. It seems the most feasible route, it's open ground, and not used for anything."

"Aye, that'd be the most sensible. But planners don't work with sense," her companion growled. "Oh no, they couldn't take their road across the common, where it'd upset nobody. They has to route it to come this way. An' if they have their way, their rotten road will plough straight across our nursery. Right through the rose gardens, and straight through the middle of Mr. Giles' house," he told her bluntly.

CHAPTER FOUR

"I DON'T need a doctor. He couldn't make a neater job of it than Pip's already done," Giles protested. "All I need is a good cup of tea. One of your specials from the big brown pot," he coaxed, and Betsy gave way.

"Well, if you won't, you won't," she grumbled, reaching for the pot from the shelf, and with her other hand automatically grasping the green felt kettle-holder with the embroidered flowers scattered in brightly coloured lazy daisy stitch across the middle, a product of a recent sale of work in the village. The kettle holder was a necessity, as Betsy wouldn't use an electric kettle, and the handle of her present one grew hot against the open fire.

"I'm afeared them electric things will blow up or something," she declared, sticking stubbornly to her blackened utensil with the green-painted lid that sat on the blackleaded trivet, singing gently in front of the glowing logs. It was a homely, companionable sound, and one that Pip had come to enjoy since she arrived at the cottage.

"I said something would happen," Betsy declared to the room in general, tipping a stream of scalding water on to the generous helping of tea. "I knew it when the smoke came down the chimney."

"At least we can be thankful it's happened, and no one's hurt," Giles responded quietly, with no sign of laughter in his face to jibe at Betsy's superstitions. For such an ardent churchgoer, her belief in old wives' tales was surprising, though Betsy herself saw nothing strange in faith and fear running side by side, and Giles respected her outlook even if he didn't necessarily condone it.

"Come on in, George," Betsy called as the foreman's head appeared round the doorway. "There's a seat on the rug if you can't find a chair," she told him comfortably, and Pip smiled. Sam's wife might not have benefited from too much schooling, but her sound common sense gave her a quick insight into the needs of other human beings that could not be bettered by a trained psychologist. She had gathered them all into her warm kitchen. Her husband, who had come hurrying at the first sound of the crash, apprehensive for Skippy's safety; Giles, who occupied the stool in the corner, and whose face was now closer to its normal healthy hue; and George, settling himself on the rug next to Giles, with his back supported by the brown-painted door of the kitchen cupboard, gathering between his knees a contented Skippy, who seemed to have forgotten all about her hazardous adventure, and was trying to make room for Punch to join her in her privileged spot. Stella and Pip sat by the table helping Betsy to prepare the much needed cup of tea. Pip milked the line of cups and thrust them along the scrubbed wooden top to her companion.

"Sugar and stir, will you, Stella? And put two in Giles' cup," she suggested.

"I don't take. . . ."

"You needn't, in your second cup," Pip ignored his protest. "Drink the first one sweet, it'll help."

"Do as teacher says." Stella handed him his cup, her black eyes laughing into his, though whether she was laughing at Giles or at Pip it was difficult to say, and Pip's lips compressed. Stella had made it sound as if she was being bossy, which was the last thing she intended, particularly to Giles. When you were only five feet and a bit, as he had reminded her, you didn't boss people who'd said goodbye to a mere six feet years ago, and o whom you already stood in considerable awe. She turned away, replacing the milk jug on the table, and met Betsy's look. A frown creased her landlady's usually

63

placid forehead, and she spoke up firmly.

"Miss Pip's right, and you know it." She, too, had recognised the need to ease their shock and fright, recognised the value of the bright fire and the small, cosy room, the "safe" feel of her own motherly, bustling presence to a group of grown-ups whose adult poise had been rudely shaken by Skippy's narrow escape.

"The gauze is coming adrift from your cut." The plaster hadn't quite stuck down, and Pip rose to her feet.

"It'll do as it is." Giles' voice was not encouraging. "I'll cope myself, if necessary," and she sat back on her seat, feeling snubbed.

"Don't be a bear, even if you have got a sore head." Stella wasn't daunted by his tone, she rose and tucked the end of the wadding firmly under the plaster, and Giles sat patiently without moving until she had finished her ministrations, which considering she had only got to stick the plaster down took her an age in time, thought Pip scathingly.

"Thanks." Giles rose to his feet, his face impassive, though he didn't snap at Stella as Pip half expected him to. As he would have done to her, she thought ruefully. "Let's go and see to that greenhouse, George, before it collapses on its own. Coming, Sam?" He turned to Betsy and smiled. "Thanks for the tea, Betsy, it was just what we all needed," he nodded, scrupulously polite as he always was to the elderly woman, despite the fact that his head must be hurting him. He'd have a marathon headache later on, Pip guessed, and her conscience smote her for labelling him ill-humoured. She hadn't known about the road.

"I'll help you wash these." She lingered in the kitchen, letting Stella go, though before the door closed behind the other girl's back she heard Giles refuse to let her accompany the men.

"I'd be happier if you were safely out of reach of any

falling glass." He was still polite, but his voice brooked no disobedience, and Stella had the wit to do as she was told. Pip saw her making for her own quarters of the nursery, and rubbed the spotless glass cloth over a wet cup thoughtfully.

"I didn't know the road was planned to come through the nursery, Betsy. I knew there was to be a bypass, of course, I've heard it mentioned now and then, but why through the nursery grounds?"

"It's the shortest route, miss." Ask a silly question, thought Pip. "If it goes round the other side of the village, across the common, and misses the nursery, it puts on a good five miles or so. It's money, you see, miss. Road building costs a lot."

"They'll have to pay in money or kind." Pip's indignation rose at the thought of Giles' lovely old home being bulldozed to make way for traffic. No wonder she'd rarely seen him smile. "And I thought he was just grumpy," she confessed.

"Not Mr. Giles, miss." Betsy looked shocked. "Why, a sweeter tempered lad you couldn't find, normally." She rose up in defence of her employer, whom Pip suspected she regarded more as a son, and certainly not as a grown-up, if her use of expression was any guide to her outlook. "Though I admit he's not been himself since them planner folk started," she sighed.

"It's funny no one's mentioned the possibility of it coming through here." Pip was puzzled.

"Well, it all started a long time before you came here," Betsy said complacently, "and folk tend to put it at the back of their minds once the first fuss has died down. Mr. Giles is fighting it, of course, he's got the local M.P. on his side and all sorts of other important folk." A stabilised pecking order was as much a part of Betsy as her superstitions. "It was a nine days' wonder when it started, but when nothing happened straight away folks forgot about it, and Mr. Giles didn't encourage them to talk about it, nor us neither," she explained simply. "Said it was better not, it only unsettled the staff in the nursery, and he was right enough there," she remembered. "When it first started most of the women said they were going to leave and get jobs in the town. We can't afford to let that happen, can we?" She included Pip in the hierarchy of the business. "There's not all that many folk round here that we can get other labour to replace folk who leave."

"No, I can understand that, and of course I won't discuss it either. I do hope everything comes out allright. Maybe Stella knows how things are going on?" There was no reason why she should, any more than the rest of the staff, except that she was the sort of woman a man might confide in, and she seemed to be on much better terms with Giles than herself.

"I doubt it, Miss Garvey isn't interested in anything but what concerns herself, and I misdoubt her business is odd enough at times." Betsy never called her Miss Stella, using her Christian name, as she did with Pip.

"Can I go to Uncle George, Gran?" Skippy was getting restless at being confined to the kitchen.

"No, that you can't. There's too much glass about." Betsy was adamant.

"But I shan't get in the way." Her voice had the beginnings of a wail, and Pip intervened hurriedly.

"Come with me, instead. If you go back to the greenhouse, Punch will follow you and he'll end up with cut paws. You wouldn't want that, would you?" She touched on the one spot calculated to deter Skippy from following the foreman anyway. She doted on the dog. "I'm going to finish that picture I showed you the other day – you know, the one with the girl and boy dancing on a flower bed. I'm going to make them in flowers after Easter," she confided. "There'll be lots of tulips and things I can use then, but I don't know what colours to put in," she added slyly.

"Oh, Punch and me'll help you." The idea caught

Skippy's interest, and she reached for the dog's collar. "They're the ones I helped you with when I danced," she remembered.

"They're the ones," agreed Pip. "You gave me the whole idea, really," she said generously, basely using the fact to keep the child at her side, and receiving her grandmother's nod of permission over the coppery curls. "This would be better in colour, easier to follow," she said thoughtfully later, regarding the finished sketch with its meticulously outlined areas numbered to correspond with a colour and flower index which she had printed below.

"Mr. Giles has got some paints," Skippy offered the information casually. "He lets me lend them now and then."

"Borrow them," Pip corrected her automatically, but Skippy's idea might be a way out for her. She didn't want to go into the market town for colours, and the one shop the village boasted would hardly have the sort of thing she required. It seemed as if Giles kept a child's painting box for Skippy to play with at odd times, and it would serve her purpose very well if he would let her borrow it. "I'll ask him for it when he gets back from the greenhouse," she told her young informant, and hoped that Giles would be as willing to lend it to her as he was to Skippy. Since it was for nursery work she didn't see why he should have any objection, but Giles' manner towards her was usually unpredictable, and the habit she had acquired since she arrived at the nursery, of avoiding him whenever possible, did not make it any easier for her to ask a favour of him now, though the realisation that the finished sketch which she had transposed on to a very large sheet of paper could be pinned on the wall and give her the information she required at a glance, as well as leaving her plenty of room for the physical work of making the frames and then eventually covering them with the living material she had to use, removed any scruples she might have had about disturbing him after dinner that evening.

"And I won't ask him how his head is, either," she vowed, remembering his curt tone earlier, but her resolution melted when he answered the door to her knock, and she saw his shadowed eyes that spoke eloquently of the headache she had guessed would overtake him.

"It was predictable," he answered her enquiry drily. "A night's sleep will cure it. But you didn't come to enquire about my head," he guessed accurately, stepping aside to allow her through the door.

"Skippy said you'd be able to let me have some paints. Or crayons would do," Pip explained her errand. "It doesn't matter if it's only a child's paintbox, I just want quickly recognisable colour areas on a wall chart to guide me when I'm working."

"You sound as if you're well organised," he approved. "You can borrow whatever you need, but they're not children's paints. Through here," he directed her through a door to the side of the hall, into a room she had never seen before. It was smaller than the drawing room, with a large window facing north, and a smaller window with leaded panes which Pip guessed faced due west. As a room it had all the advantages, she thought – the clear hard north light for reading and writing, and the cheerfulness of the sun through the leaded window to lighten the hours the occupant spent there, either busy at the large oak desk on which some papers were scattered as if Giles had been studying them when she knocked at the door, a slim fountain pen uncapped across them, or relaxed in the deep hide chair that stood handily beside the well filled bookcase. It was obviously the room Giles used as a study, and Pip looked about her interestedly. A favourite room so often took on the character of its owner, and this one had a quiet strength about it that was immediately appealing, and was a reflection of what she knew of Giles.

A covered easel in the corner of the north-facing window caught her eye, and she glanced from it to the man, a question in her eyes.

"The paints I give Skippy to play with aren't children's things," he repeated. "I let her have any tubes of colour that are nearly spent, and give her one of my old brushes and some sheets of paper. She and I often sit and paint together," he smiled. "There's her easel in the corner." He indicated a small easel carrying a sheet of paper daubed with a futuristic-looking mixture of violent oranges and purples. "She likes bright colours," he explained gravely, "and it keeps her from under Betsy's feet now and then. You never know, it might spark off an interest in art, later on."

"I didn't know. . . ." There was a lot Pip didn't know about Giles Shieldon, she realised, and wondered why the thought caused a small ache to start inside her.

"I don't do as much painting as I'd like to." He turned towards the big easel casually. "There isn't a lot of time to spare, with the nursery to run, so I content myself with illustrating our yearly catalogue."

So Giles was responsible for the colour plates in the Shieldon catalogue that Pip had admired so much. She had assumed that his publisher had set them up. They were each a small work of art, and she did not wonder that the catalogue ran out of print so quickly. Stella had managed to rescue a copy for her to look at when she first joined the staff.

"I can't see what there is to make such a fuss about," the dark-haired girl's lack of interest was abysmal. "I'd rather read a fashion mag myself. But everyone to their own taste," she conceded, throwing the copy across to Pip at dinner one night. The recipient found it very much to her taste. Two of the pictures she immediately put into plain frames, and they graced her bedroom wall. Was this another, on the easel?

"You seem to like roses as much as I do, so you may be

interested in the one I'm doing now." Giles pulled the cover away from the easel and switched on a reading lamp so that the light fell softly on to the canvas. It revealed a single rose, newly opened from the bud, its still tightly furled heart deeply pink with the clear delicacy of a baby's soft cheeks, or the first awakening of a dawn sky. The outer petals curled gracefully away, cupping the centre in a close embrace as if reluctant to allow it to open too soon, their colour shading to a delicate cream at the tips, the transformation so skilfully accomplished by the artist that the rose might indeed have been freshly plucked from one of the nursery bushes. It was so real that Pip could almost catch the perfume. Wonderingly she traced a finger along the stem, strongly depicted; even the thorns showed sharply defined, and with a clear green mossing such as she had not seen since the days when she had been allowed to play in her grandmother's garden in the far north, that treasure house of all such old-fashioned loveliness that seemed to have died away along with her generation.

"It's years since I've seen a moss rose." Her delight showed in her face. "I didn't know you grew them here?"

"I don't, not in the nursery, though I still grow some in my own private garden, in the walled part." Pip had never seen inside the walled garden, though Betsy had told her that Giles kept it much as it had always been since the place was a monastery, steadfastly refusing to alter what had been laid out before even his ancestors were thought of, by dedicated men who grew to serve their own needs, and those of others who came to them for help. According to her landlady, there was no herb for which she could ask to garnish her wide repertoire of dishes or medicaments with which she treated her family that Giles could not supply. She had often seen him disappear through the wooden, arch-shaped doorway in the wall, sometimes with his personal visitors, but more often on his own, as if in the brief moments of his spare time he treasured the privacy of his own particular sanctuary, allowing only those particularly close to him the privilege of entry. Skippy and Punch had carte blanche to come and go as they pleased, and the child had offered to take her there when she expressed an interest one day, but though Pip had often longed to follow the little girl through the doorway in the wall, the thought of the reaction of her employer if he discovered her trespassing was enough to daunt the most intrepid, and even Pip's love of gardens, in particular old or unusual ones, did not give her the courage to breach the gate.

"Is this going to be in your next season's catalogue?" She tore her fascinated gaze away from the canvas.

"No," Giles sounded oddly hesitant, "it isn't a real rose, at least not yet. It's only a – a – dream. . . ."

"You're breeding a rose of your own?" Intuitively she grasped his meaning.

"Yes," he nodded. "I've been experimenting for years. This June the bushes should give the blooms I've been working for." He stopped abruptly, and Pip saw his lips tighten.

"You'll see the blooms before they start on the new road." She spoke gently, impulsively, her sympathy vivid in her expression, and Giles' lips tilted in a slight smile, lopsided and bitter, but a smile nevertheless.

"That's about the only consolation I've got."

"You'll have the rose." To Pip that seemed a precious possession, a rose of your very own, bred by your own hands and nurtured to perfection from the most perfect material. "Have you given it a name?" She turned back to the canvas, seeking a title, but there was none to see.

"No, I'm going to enter it for the County Show, make it the focal point of our exhibition there, and name it then. I hope, when it's won the rose bowl – that's the first prize," he explained. "It's everything a rose should be," his face in the lamplight was afire with enthusiasm. "I've crossed and recrossed to give it all that's best in the strain.

It's a vigorous grower, the stock of bushes I've got already shows that."

"And?" Pip's interest was obvious, and drew a ready response from the man beside her. He seemed to have forgotten for the moment who she was and what she had come for, temporarily it was kind talking to kind, and nothing else mattered.

"It's been bred to be rain and disease-resistant," he explained seriously, lapsing into technicalities, "and the blooms when they come should be a good shape, and sweetly perfumed."

"Heavens, poor thing!" Pip laughed. "And on top of all that it's still got to have a name!"

What would he name it? she wondered. Or perhaps, nearer to the mark, who would he name it after? The obvious thing would be to name his rose after a wife or a mother, but Giles was single, and according to Betsy neither of his parents was still alive. A girl-friend? Pip had seen no sign of one, and Giles rarely seemed to go out, certainly not regularly, which would indicate a close liaison.

"Some time you must see my experimental rose garden." He didn't say when, just some time. Like the invitations to "drop in and see us if you're ever our way" that one gets from holiday acquaintances, kindly meant, but insincere, and not meant to be taken seriously.

"Thank you. . . ." Pip felt oddly disappointed, suddenly let down in some curious fashion, and Giles gave her a quick glance, sensing her withdrawal. "I'll look out some paints for you." He turned away and opened a wall cupboard behind the easel, producing a neat box of paints and a smaller one which contained a selection of brushes.

"They're fresh tubes?" Pip took them from him hesitantly, casting knowledgeable eyes over his offering. She herself didn't paint, she preferred sketching; it was simpler to carry the materials with her when she was

72

walking, a block and a pencil could be stowed easily in a pocket, and paints were not so readily transportable, but she knew enough about their use to make a workmanlike job of anything which she undertook, which was all that she required for the project she had in hand.

"You didn't think I'd treat you the same as Skippy, and give you my spent tubes?" He smiled amusedly. "From the look of your sketching I assumed you'd know how to handle paints as well." He had paid her the highest compliment of any craftsman, that of handing over his best tools.

"I'll treat them carefully," she promised.

"I wouldn't give them to you if I thought otherwise."

She made considerable inroads into quite a few of his new tubes of paints, she realised several days later. Her wall chart was a large one, and she became so absorbed that time flew by without her even noticing the number of hours she spent in its creation.

"Ooh, it's lovely!" sighed Skippy from the rug, circling thin arms about her drawn-up knees.

"It's only a tool really, for me to use when I'm making up the real thing in flowers." Pip had explained her object in making the chart, and living in the environment of the nursery the six-year-old readily understood her reasoning, though the magnet of the coloured picture that had grown under Pip's busy brush had drawn her to the artist's side for hours at a time, much to her grandmother's relief, since repairs to the damaged greenhouse had been extensive, and the work going on there would otherwise have attracted the attention of the child and exposed her to possible danger.

"Then you won't want it after your job's done?" The pixie face was solemn, her grandmother's strict training forbidding its owner to put into words the boon that her beseeching gaze implored.

"No, I shan't want the picture afterwards, though I'll save it for you, if you like, when I've finished with it."

Pip smiled down at her small companion, well rewarded for her thoughtful offer by the sheer delight that sprang into the freckled face.

"Oh, yes. Yes, *please*!" Skippy breathed. "Gran. . . ." She fled to tell her grandmother the wonderful news, and Pip laid down the paints with a sigh, conscious now her chart was finished that she had spent overlong hours cramped in one position, and conscious also that the chart, which had started out as a purely functional exercise, had somehow become a very attractive picture, despite her previous protests of lack of skill as an artist.

"It must be Giles' posh paints," she told herself out loud, pleased that it had turned out so well, if only for Skippy's sake.

"In that case you'd better keep them, if they encourage you to do that sort of work," a voice behind her suggested, and she spun round, the damp brushes still clutched in her hand. "Skippy just tore in to tell us she's going to acquire a masterpiece," Giles explained his presence, "so I thought I'd better come and have a look at such a gift for myself."

Pip gave him a long look, uncertain whether or not he was being sarcastic, but she saw nothing but interest in his lean brown face.

"I'll clean your brushes and let you have them all back." She dropped them into a handy jamjar on the table beside her, and rubbed her pink-stained fingers with a paint-spattered rag. "I wanted to get it finished so that I can start constructing the frames after Easter. Heavens – Easter! I haven't got Skippy's egg yet," she realised with dismay, "nor her toffee bar for helping me. Oh my goodness! That only leaves Saturday. . . ."

"I'm going into Mossly this morning, I'll give you a lift in if you like, though I can't promise to give you one back home."

"I'll jump on the bus back if I can only get into town. Can you wait for a few minutes while I clean up?" she asked him, anxious not to delay him and probably make him wish he hadn't made the offer in the first place. Giles' moods were too uncertain to be tampered with, and although she now knew the cause to be worry over the proposed new road, and the safety of his nursery, she was nevertheless anxious not to upset him. "I need to go in and check a measurement at the Manor Hotel," she told him, "I can do that at the same time and collect a chocolate egg on the way back. I suppose I could have asked Stella, she said she was going into Mossly, but I don't know when she'll be back." Or whether she would be willing to carry shopping, which was the main reason she hadn't asked. Stella's assignments in town were not usually of a nature that she would want to be embarrassed by parcels.

"I'll be late coming back, I expect." Giles checked his speed as they reached the end of the nursery road and approached the junction with the lane. "I . . . idiot!" he roared through the open driving window as he accelerated, and then instantly braked hard, tossing Pip to the limit of her seat belt. She closed her eyes as a red sports car hurtled round the bend, well on the wrong side of the road, and missed their front bumper by the thickness of a scrape of paint. She felt their own vehicle rock with the wind of its passing, and opened her eyes in time to see it vanish with more haste than caution over the rise of the next hill.

"Phew!" She let out her breath with a sigh of relief, and cupped both her hands over her ears as Giles gave a pithy description of the other driver's possible ancestry to the disappearing cloud of dust.

"You can unstop them now, the all clear's sounded." A firm finger hooked her hand down, and she slewed a wary glance at her driver. He confronted her with a grin which broadened at the patent relief on her face when she saw his fury was spent.

"Call it intense provocation," he excused himself. "I

don't usually let fly like that."

"It was too close for comfort," Pip forgave him.

"Closer than I like, with a passenger in the car," he admitted. "If he wants to break his own silly neck that's his affair," he glared after the other driver. "Another two seconds and his bonnet would have been on your lap," he realised, his jaw tightening, and disregarding the fact that his own lap would have undoubtedly shared the burden, to the detriment of its wellbeing. Pip warmed to his consideration, and settled herself back in her seat contentedly, enjoying his firm handling of the vehicle, conscious that she felt no sign of the nerves that afflict most drivers who find themselves in the passenger seat, and would have been excusable in herself after the narrow escape they had just experienced.

It was only when they were nearing Mossly, leaving the narrow, twisting lanes behind, and joining the flow of traffic into the small market town, that Pip remembered Giles' remark about his time of return that night. Late, he'd said. He'd been going to say something else as well, but the incident with the sports car had stopped him from enlarging, even if he intended to. She noticed for the first time that he was dressed up. He always looked smart, but these were definitely not working clothes. The cut of his suit, in fine brown tweed, hinted at a select origin, as did the quality of the pale cream shirt and warmly coloured cashmere tie that picked up the slight fleck visible in the tweed. He must have an appointment in town, thought Pip, that would be the reason he couldn't bring her back.

"I'll drop you here, you can make your own way in." The Manor Hotel loomed in front of them, breaking into Pip's train of thought, and Giles pulled into the forecourt, though he kept his engine running as if he intended to go on elsewhere. Pip heard him accelerate as she ran up the hotel steps, but when she turned round to wave he had disappeared, and she had no idea which direction he took. The drive in to the Manor was round a circular shrubbery, which also led to the car park at the back, and he could have gone either way. A few minutes later she was too busy to bother about Giles or anything else except the job she had come to do.

"Help yourself," the proprietor answered her request for permission to take her missing measurements. "Go anywhere you want to," he waved an expansive hand at the hotel in general.

"Just the ballroom. I'd forgotten to gauge height for some figures I intend putting in the space in front of the orchestra. I don't want to hide the M.C.," Pip smiled.

"That would never do," the owner of the Manor agreed gravely, nodding appreciation as Pip explained her purpose. "It sounds wonderful," he enthused, "right out of the ordinary, although one expects that from Shieldons – you do tend to have an individual touch." Pip didn't know whether he meant herself or the nursery, but she felt pleased at his unexpected compliment nevertheless.

"I'd thought of putting the nursery shield, mounted in flowers, behind the top table for the dinner. Would you have space?" Pip had no idea what room the maitre d'hotel would require to accommodate the tables, and whether there would be space sufficient for a trestle to take a floral shield of the size she had in mind.

"That would be most appropriate. Tell me what space you need, and I'll adjust the table arrangements accordingly," her companion was all enthusiasm.

"Fairly big." Pip stood on tiptoe and indicated approximate areas with widespread arms. "If it's supported on a table about the same height as your dining tables, I thought it would frame the principal guests against a fairly unusual background. Good for photography," she explained. "I understand the Lord Mayor will be there."

"Indeed he will," the proprietor confirmed, "and of course Mr. Shieldon will be in his usual place, so it will be doubly appropriate, having the shield where you suggest."

Betsy had said something similar when Pip wondered aloud where Giles would sit at the function. "In his usual place," she had said.

"And where is his usual place?"

"At the top table, of course." Her companion looked slightly shocked. "Mr. Shieldon will be one of the principal guests," he emphasized. "The fact that he's giving the flowers is purely incidental."

She should have guessed, of course. She was so accustomed to regarding Giles as her boss, owner of the Shieldon Rose Nurseries, and a highly successful business man, that it was easy to overlook the fact that he was the scion of a family that dated back to Cromwell's time. It wasn't easy to imagine the reserved, rather solitary person she was accustomed to moving in the restricted circle of county social life, and she imagined he had little taste for it, probably preferring individual friendships as she did herself, from whatever walk of life they came, looking for, and finding, kinship with like-minded fellow human beings.

"We're not often lucky enough to persuade Mr. Shieldon to attend these functions," the proprietor of the Manor said in a satisfied tone, unwittingly confirming her guess, "but of course he's a busy man." Was it work, or lack of inclination that kept Giles away? Pip wondered. She suspected the latter. "Ah well, he usually comes out once or twice a year, mostly to charity functions, and of course he's particularly interested in helping to get this pool for the hospital. D'you know," he waxed confidential, "we've already sold most of the tickets. I don't think Mr. Shieldon knows that yet. Why, there he is, just going into the dining room," he exclaimed. "I'll let him know, I'm sure he'll be pleased. Unless you're joining him for lunch?" He looked at Pip enquiringly, rather doubtfully, she thought with an inward smile, since she was hardly in suitable dress for lunching here. Her cherry red trouser suit and white, high-necked sweater were both gay and functional, and extremely smart, but it was hardly what she would have chosen to wear if she was lunching with Giles at the Manor.

"No, I'm not joining him," she denied, watching from the seclusion of the ballroom as Giles' tall figure passed through the opened double doors of the main dining room, paused courteously as the head waiter came hurrying, then turned as if to ask his companion if the offered table met with her approval. That it was a woman Pip could see by the sheerly stockinged legs and clinging skirt that were just visible behind the pillar of the doorway. Unconsciously she frowned, her memory teased by something familiar about the garment, something that she recognised quickly enough as its owner stepped into full view, and Stella Garvey slipped a proprietorial hand through Giles' arm, her dark head tilted back and her black eyes smiling up into his as he bent his head to say something that must have been significant to draw the light peal of laughter that came clearly back to Pip from his lovely companion.

CHAPTER FIVE

PIP was several yards past the confectioners before she remembered Skippy's Easter egg, and by the time she had retraced her steps and made her purchases, she had to run to catch the bus that took her to within a mile of the nursery gates.

She felt curiously depressed as she alighted at the bus stop at the corner of the lane, and watched her transport disappear round the bend of the main road, leaving her standing on her own. The lane beside her climbed the hill on her left, and she turned into it, slowing her steps as it rose steeply towards the spinney at the top, and the gate where she had sat and eaten her chocolate bar. She would have liked to sit on it now and rest for a while, but she remembered the splinter that had snagged her working trousers, and resisted the temptation to stop there again. She did not want to risk tearing her trouser suit, which was fairly new, so she kept walking, thankful that her parcels were lightweights.

Normally a walk cheered her up whatever her mood, but today her well-tried panacea failed her, and she wished she had stayed in Mossly for a while, window-shopping as she had originally intended to; the bustling life among the stores might have lightened her depression, but the thought of meeting Giles and Stella had driven her away. Giles had said he would probably return late to the nursery, so they must be intending to spend the afternoon together, probably remaining there for a dinner and a show. Stella hadn't mentioned she was going with Giles. She had said it would be interesting to try and rouse their employer, and despite their normal lack of communication Pip thought Stella would not have resisted gloating over the fact that she had succeeded.

She despised the crudeness of the other girl's deliberate campaign. If she had employed such tactics on the type of man she usually chose for an escort Pip would have wasted no sympathy, but to deliberately set out to entice Giles for no other reason than casual amusement seemed to her to be indefensible. To play with love was the privilege of the very young, whose transient attachments left no deep scar on untried hearts, but taught them by pain the price of wayward affection, while it yet had no lasting power to hurt, leaving the wise among them to reap the rich reward of something fine and strong that could only be bought by waiting, and paid for by a lifetime of giving, that to the truly blessed seemed but a lifetime of receiving, so deep is the joy that gives the heart calm anchorage whatever storms might temporarily toss life's surface. Pip felt her anger rise against Stella, that she should use Giles so; he was too fine for such treatment. She told herself in vain that it was no business of hers, Giles was a grown man and quite capable of looking after himself, but the anger remained, and she turned to work to try and settle herself down. There was plenty to do, and the girl she was training was glad enough of help with the wedding bouquets that had been ordered for the coming holiday.

"It looks as if the vicar's going to have a busy weekend."

Her assistant smiled at her pleasantry, and offered a confidence.

"I'm hoping to make my own bouquet this time next year, miss." She looked out of the window and caught sight of the passing figure of George, with Skippy in tow as usual, and offered another. "I reckon someone else will want one too, and that before long," her eighteen-year-old wisdom concluded, and Pip hid a smile.

"It must be catching," she replied gravely, trying to still the small knot of misery inside her that had persisted ever since she watched Giles and Stella walk into the hotel dining room together. "If you keep on like this," she silently told the knot, "I shall think I'm jealous."

"Well, aren't you?" it just as silently replied.

"Pass me the wire," she told her assistant briskly. "I'll help you with the last of these flowers, then you can get off early," she suggested, to the evident delight of her companion, whose bright engagement ring flashed a cheerful accompaniment to her busy hands. The work helped to calm Pip, stilling for a while the argument that seemed to be going on inside her whether she liked it or not, the sort of argument that children have when they are blowing dandelion clocks, of the "yes, you are, no, I'm not," variety. Pip felt herself to be helplessly trapped in the middle of a ding-dong battle, that when she stamped on it with all her willpower stopped for a moment or two, but it always seemed to stop on the "yes, you are" side of the argument. When the flowers were finished, bouquets for other brides who Pip hoped wistfully felt happier than she did at the moment, there was no barrier against her thoughts, which had their way with a ruthless cruelty that sent her flying to the sanctuary of her bedroom long before she would normally have retired, seeking the cloak of darkness that she discovered brought neither sleep nor respite, since it could not quieten the voice within her that still insisted "yes, you are" as she eventually dozed off.

The sound of a car woke her and she automatically looked at the clock. The luminous hands said ten-thirty, which didn't seem late to her, though it sounded like Giles' vehicle. She heard it stop at the front of the house, heard the door slam, then a little while later the engine started up again and droned away in the direction of the old stables, which Giles now used as a garage for his own vehicle and the nursery vans. It was well after midnight when she heard the door to Stella's flat slam shut, with the girl's usual lack of consideration for anyone else on the premises who might be asleep. The walls of the cottage were thick, but through the open window Pip could hear a snatch of the latest pop music coming from Stella's quarters, as if she had been dancing, and the music still ran through her head. Pip knew she hadn't been mistaken in the time she heard Giles' car come in, so presumably he had taken Stella with him into his house, probably to have supper together beside the fire. She wondered if Giles had shown her his painting of the rose and unreasonably hoped that he hadn't. For that brief few minutes when he had shown it to Pip they had found themselves two people in complete accord, their love of roses a common ground wherein they both walked and found it good.

Deliberately she avoided Stella the next morning, and sought refuge in her work, unable to face the other girl when her own feelings were still so aroused, and fearing that her anger might drive her into speaking her mind, and so make her own position in the nursery untenable. She would hate to have to leave and turn her back on a promising career – and on Giles, her treacherous heart reminded her, and miserably she let it have its say, acknowledging that it spoke the truth, however hurtful that might be.

"I'll have to give you a refund on the money you pay me for your keep." Betsy broke the silence as she served dinner to the two girls that evening. "Miss Garvey out for lunch and dinner yesterday, and you not eating your meals," she scolded gently.

"Did you have a good time?" Pip felt obliged to ask, though with her new self-knowledge she shrank from the answer. If Stella had enjoyed herself it meant that Giles had, too, and enjoyed Stella's company into the bargain.

"Yes, I – I think I did."

83

Pip stared across the table, wondering if she had heard right. When Stella condescended to describe her evenings out, which wasn't very often, she was usually a lot more emphatic. She never seemed to have "a nice time", her evenings were always "hilarious" or "stupendous" or "fantastic". This half-hesitant admission sounded as if she really meant it. Her descriptions usually sounded as if they were meant to convince Stella as much as her audience. Pip noticed with surprise that she wasn't smoking, which was practically the first time since she had known her that she had seen her without a cigarette in her fingers. She had lit one out of pure habit when she came in to dinner, but it smouldered unnoticed on the ashtray by her place setting, the long tube of ash lying undisturbed across the china tray. And she seemed more relaxed, somehow, thought Pip critically, driven into a new awareness by the force of her own feelings. The tense, nervous movements that she had always associated with Stella since they become colleagues were no longer visible. She lounged relaxed in her chair and regarded Pip with a thoughtful look that had no hint in it of the usual malice that seemed to lace most of her actions, a restless, unsatisfied tilting at life in general that managed to keep most people at bay, including Pip, who had early in their acquaintanceship deemed discretion the better part of valour and contented herself with remaining at arms' length, although it went against her own friendly nature.

She began to wish she had made plans to go home for Easter, despite the amount of work she had to do; at least it would get her away from the nursery – and from Giles – for a while, and give her time to think. She had desired to avoid Giles before, but for a very different reason; then her wish had a single-mindedness of purpose actuated by her dislike of him, but now she was torn between a need to go and an equally strong urge to remain, so that while she could not be with him, she could at least be in his vicinity. It looked like being a drab Easter, she thought wretchedly.

"You don't look like having much company this Easter." Stella spoke as if reading her thoughts, and Pip started. Stella never had been any company for her, she had been antagonistic to Pip from the start, and made no attempt to hide the fact. They usually only met about the nursery premises, when work claimed their attention and precluded any opportunity for social contact, or at mealtimes, and even then only briefly. Stella never managed to get up on time in the mornings, so Pip had usually finished her breakfast before the other girl appeared. Betsy insisted on serving to time, her disapproval of the other girl's inconsiderate ways an open bone of contention between them. Lunch was usually a snack on the job, often in Pip's case miles away from the nursery, and at dinner time Stella swallowed her food in hasty silence, urgent to be away so that she could meet one or another of her doubtful escorts. She openly said she didn't care for women's company, so Pip withdrew into herself, not caring to trespass when she patently was not wanted, but now there seemed to be an odd hint of curiosity in her eyes as she regarded Pip across the table, for once seemingly in no hurry to be finished.

"Oh, I shall be busy most of the time," Pip answered her casually. "There's a massive amount of preparation work to do for this event at the Manor Hotel, and I promised to take Skippy on to the common with her kite," she added, making it sound as if she considered Easter wouldn't be long enough for all she had to pack into it, whereas her main concern would be to keep out of Giles' way, if he intended to remain at home.

"I'll be away for a day or two. Giles will, too," she added with a return of her old swordsmanship.

Pip started, caught off guard, and a gleam of amusement shone for a moment in her fellow diner's black eyes, as if they held some unguessed secret. Hastily she averted her own for fear they might betray her, she was unused to guarding her thoughts, and the last thing she wanted was to expose herself to Stella's sly taunts. Shame at her own relief in seeing her colleague ready to go away the next morning made her offer to help with her suitcases to the car, which was pulled up outside the door.

"I thought you were only going away for Easter?" She viewed the two suitcases and the stuffed holdall with surprise.

"I'll be away for about five days," Stella looked over her baggage casually. "I don't like my evening gowns crushed. And besides, I shan't have to carry them," she said indifferently.

"I should hope not, all this lot." Giles appeared through the door. "Ready now?" He picked up the two cases, and tucked the holdall under one arm. "I'm off now, Betsy," he called, and nodded in a friendly manner to Pip. She felt his look rest on her face, as if he waited for some comment from her, and she quickly turned away, afraid that her face might reveal her thoughts. When she looked again Giles was busy stowing the luggage in the boot of his car, and Pip remained by the door, wishing she could go in, but it would look rude not to see them off. Giles handed Stella into the passenger seat, carefully making sure her coat was tucked in after her before he slammed the door. When he had given Pip a lift into Mossly she had managed the task of getting into the car by herself, she thought waspishly, but honesty made her admit that that wasn't Stella's fault. She raised her hand in answer to Giles' wave – Stella didn't bother to turn round – and shut the cottage door on the retreating car feeling as if she had said goodbye to more than two Easter holidaymakers. Something of what she felt must have shown; for Betsy gave her a keen look.

"Take Skippy with you for company," she offered her a quick solution to the empty seat beside her in the van that was stood ready for her to deliver the bouquets she had made up the night before, and when Pip eventually returned to the nursery she was feeling a good deal more cheerful, thanks to the chattering company she had on the journey.

"She's all yours now, George," she handed her small charge over to the foreman. "Oh, by the way, I'll need some good thick wire for tomorrow," she added. "I'm going to start on those frames for the decorations at the Manor. The ones for the figures of the children, and the shield, will have to carry quite a weight, so I'll need something fairly tough."

"I've got plenty of wire, miss, but do you think you'll manage? It's a bit on the thick side." The foreman looked doubtfully at Pip's small hands.

"I'll cope," she said confidently, but the sight of the gauge of the wire roll that appeared in her workshop the next morning gave her some doubts. It was ideal for the job she had in mind, just what she needed in fact, but. . . . She tried it tentatively, and realised that she would need a stouter pair of pliers. She started on the outline of the girl figure first, to get used to the feel of it. The outline of the crinoline skirt was easy enough, the bends were gradual, but when she came to the top part of the figure, the outflung arms, and the old-fashioned bonnet, the twists required were sharper. Even with the heavier tool it took the strength of both hands to achieve the effect she desired. She held the outline against the full-sized painting pinned to the wall, and looked at it critically. To anyone else it would probably have looked perfect, but it did not meet Pip's exacting standards, and she gave an exclamation of annoyance.

"Bother! I'll have to use a hammer."

"I'll get you one, if you like."

"Oh yes, please, George. The wire's ideal, but I'm finding it a bit hard going . . . oh!"

"It isn't George, it's me. But I'll get you the hammer if you want me to, just the same." Giles stood in the doorway regarding her with amusement written all over his face, and she flushed angrily. She would have done anything rather than admit to him that she was defeated by a piece of wire, but it was too late now. He'd heard, and seen – his standards were as high as her own, and his keen eyes took in the wired outline with a knowledgeable glance that she knew missed nothing. "You haven't managed to get the bends sharp enough, and I don't think a hammer will help, you won't be able to get the shape true. You need a stronger pair of pliers – oh, you've already got some. You need a stronger pair of wrists, in that case," he stated the obvious, realisation of her difficulty dawning on him

"I thought you'd gone away?" Pip said the first thing that came into her head, confusion at his unexpected appearance throwing her temporarily off balance. She wished he wouldn't lean against the doorpost looking at her like that, his brown gaze seemed to probe into her innermost thoughts. Well, let it, she could control those, at least while he was there. It was when she was alone they had their way, no matter how hard she tried to check them, and always they seemed to turn on Giles. The very image of him seemed emblazoned on her mind. Running from the fallen tree, with Skippy in his arms. Standing by the gate in the lane, scolding her for wasting time. And leaning now on the doorpost with an unfathomable look in his eyes that made her wonder what it was he was thinking. So long as he didn't probe her heart, that she couldn't control. It beat inside her with the insistence of native drums throbbing a message across the far reaches of primitive lands. The message her heart was sending was primitive enough, she thought. Love was as old as the human race, the hub of their universe, and the star to which they hitched the chariot of all their finest dreams.

She moved uneasily under his look, fearing lest by some sixth sense he read the message, and dreading his reaction, his normal attitude to her was curt enough, although it had altered within the last few weeks she realised, he no longer bit at her as he used to, although he still remained distant, seemingly unapproachable. Perhaps it was her own hesitancy that made her fear to approach him? Pip didn't know, and was not prepared to argue the finer points of her feelings – they were raw enough as it was. If Giles wanted Stella, let him have her. He would have to wait until she had her divorce finalised, but she doubted if he would let that stand in his way. He would wait patiently if he had to, to gain the prize he desired. As he had waited for the rose he desired, quietly working year after year to achieve his perfect bloom.

"I was only away for the one day and night." His voice held a hint of surprise, and broke in on Pip's musings, drawing her back to earth and out of the realm of her own thoughts. She returned gladly, for she found them painful companions. So was Giles, she thought wryly, but she could hardly tell him to go away and leave her alone; it was his nursery, after all. "Perhaps it's as well I came back, you can do with some help. Here, let me." He slid out of his jacket and gripped the pliers with sure fingers, measuring the shape of the wire with his eye against the shape of the painting on the wall. "You've got it nearly right, it's just the awkward bits here . . . and here," he lapsed into silent concentration, manipulating the tool skilfully, achieving just what Pip had aimed at and hadn't the strength in her wrists to accomplish.

"Why couldn't I have dreamed up something more ordinary?" she wondered with quick exasperation. "Something that I could do myself, without any help." Perversely, now that Giles was here she wished he wasn't, longing to be left alone so that she could somehow straighten out the emotional upheaval that had descended on her, and turned her ordered world upside down. And all because she had seen Stella accompany Giles into a hotel dining room. Or was it? Hadn't she felt this before, and not acknowledged it? Or perhaps not recognised it for what it was, for Pip had come to Giles heart-whole, waiting as the wise do to give it wholly and completely, or not at all. For her, no compromise would do. Hadn't the dormant seed first been germinated by the danger of the falling tree, and that awful split second of realisation that Giles might be crushed under its dreadful weight? In that second, a whole lifetime of desolation had gripped her, leaving her shaken and spent, and she had, in her ignorance, passed it off as shock. Now she knew it for what it was, and knew also that for her it must remain a rose that never blossomed, a plant to be cherished but denied the freedom to grow and the joy of eventual fulfilment.

Silently she watched him finish the shape of the girl figure, check it against the wall chart until he was satisfied with his efforts, and turn with outstretched hands, offering her the results, his look asking for her approval, though he remained silent himself.

"It's just right!" Pip made no effort to hide her pleasure, the outline of her first figure was perfect, and her delight showed in her face.

"I'll help you with your other one if you like." Giles looked pleased with the reception of his efforts. "May I?" he added unexpectedly, and Pip looked at him in surprise. She was his employee, and the job was for him, so he had no need to ask if he could help with it.

"He sounds like Stella," she thought, eyeing him wonderingly. She had been hesitant, too, and it had sounded as alien coming from her as it did from Giles.

"Of course," she stopped uncertainly. "It's catching," she thought with desperate amusement. "I'm doing it now."

"In that case, let's work together," he smiled, and Pip's heart warmed to him, her misery melting like early frost under a strengthening sun. When he smiled like that there seemed to be no barriers between them. The aloof curtness that had characterised Giles' earlier behaviour towards her, and had drawn a reaction of defensive resentment from Pip, had vanished as if it had never been, and for the first time, with the exception of those brief, elusive moments when they stood together looking at the painted figure of a rose, she felt completely relaxed in his company. Happily she reached for the wire, eager to start now on the outline of the other figure, that of a dancing boy in Dutch style trousers and baggy blouse, a floppy beret engulfing his head. Silently they worked in unison, absorbed in their joint task, Pip feeding the wire to him and Giles manipulating it into shape with deft twists of the heavy pliers. Once, their hands touched, a brief electric moment, and the man stopped work and smiled as if to encourage her. As if she needed any encouragement, working with him like this, though a glance at her watch made her realise that they had been working for over two hours, and he probably thought she was tired.

"There, I think that'll do." He gave a final decisive clip with his tool and held the outline up for her to view. She nodded dumbly, suddenly unable to speak, regretting that their brief time together was over and the rest of the work she would have to do alone. It seemed a bleak prospect now, although she had looked forward to it before. "What about props?" Giles was questioning her, and she returned to practicalities with an effort. "When those frames are covered they'll be quite a weight. They'll need something fairly sturdy to hold them." He leaned back against her workbench, arms folded, seemingly at peace with the world.

"George has got some props of various lengths. I thought I'd try them out to see which ones hold the frames best. But I want to get the wire backing on to them first, the mesh is thin and I can handle it myself," Pip added hastily, fearing lest he should think she was trying to keep him by her side. She scorned to use Stella's tactics, and pride forbade that she should detain him when he was probably urgent to be away on business of his own.

"Then you've finished with this wire?" He indicated the roll of heavy gauge material they had been using.

"Yes, George said he'd collect it and put it back in store."

"In that case tell him I took it. I've a use for some myself."

Pip opened her mouth to ask him what he wanted it for, realised her query would probably sound impertinent, and shut it again, and glanced up to meet his suddenly mysterious look that made her glad she had not displayed her curiosity. She did not have it satisfied until the next morning, at breakfast time. With Stella away, and Skippy's mother staying in the house, Pip suggested to Betsy that she should have her meals with the family to save her landlady the trouble of carrying everything into the dining room for just one person. Her offer was accepted with alacrity by that good lady, and a whoop of joy from Skippy.

"You can sit by me an' Mummy," she offered generously, wriggling her stool nearer to her parent to make room on their side of the table.

"Sure?" Pip smiled at Betsy's daughter, meeting her friendly nod of permission. "Is it all right if I take Skippy on the common this afternoon?" It was a good opportunity to ask; she knew the hours the child's mother spent at the cottage were precious to them both.

"Oh yes, miss. Skippy, go and bring in the bread, that's a good girl," she digressed, effectively removing the youngster out of earshot. "Me and George are going for a walk ourselves, this afternoon, and it'd be better if we was on our own," she said, lowering her voice. "We want to – to – talk things over, like, and if I know Skippy's with you. . . ." She stopped, confused, and Pip nodded understandingly.

"I'll take her out immediately after lunch, and we won't be back until teatime," she promised.

"That's real good of you, miss," Skippy's mother said gratefully. "You know about me an' George?" she asked with a rosy blush, and briefly Pip gripped the work-roughened hand beside her on the table.

"I'd guessed – and hoped," she confessed. "Does Skippy know?" She didn't want to say anything in front of the child that would embarrass her mother, and perhaps upset the little girl.

"Lor', yes, miss. Skippy not only knows, she reckons she's organised the whole thing," her mother laughed, her eyes twinkling merrily. When she smiled like that, she looked as carefree as her daughter. Happiness did wonderful things for people, thought Pip wistfully, and wondered what her own face looked like. She felt anything but happy right now. "George is right fond of the lass," Skippy's mother went on thankfully. "Put the loaf on the board, lovie, and come and sit down," she switched her conversation abruptly as Skippy rejoined them, and hitched the little girl closer to the table. "Reckons she's going to be a bridesmaid, this one," she confided cheerfully, ruffling the copper curls with an affectionate hand.

"Look, isn't this pretty?" Skippy's attention was taken by more immediate things, in the shape of the tinsel covering of her chocolate egg that Pip had just laid beside her breakfast plate. "An' Mr. Giles left us a present, too," she told Pip. "Isn't it a big one?" she demanded, displaying Giles' offering after breakfast was over. "It's as tall as me," she said truthfully.

"It's a beauty!" Pip gazed at the result of Giles' handiwork, her curiosity about his need for wire pleasurably satisfied. It formed the framework of a sturdy kite that had been carefully covered in stout canvas, on which was painted a delightful Disney-style bluebird with, and Pip's lips lifted, a vivid scarlet rose held in its bright

93

yellow beak. Giles and his roses! she thought, as pleased as the child. The kite must have made an irresistible canvas to him. "Skippy, it's lovely!" She hugged her delightedly. Giles had done just the thing to please the small girl at her side, and the painstaking workmanship pointed to hours of application after he left her yesterday. Making the kite must have taken a considerable time, and painting it would probably keep him up long after bedtime, she guessed shrewdly. Even the tail of the kite was meticulously made, with stiff paper bows in vivid colours; purloined, she guessed, from the nursery stores. It would look wonderful in flight. "What a gorgeous present!"

"Did you thank Mr. Giles for it?" Skippy's mother was more intent on manners than fun.

"Yes, of course I did." Skippy looked pained. "But Pip's still got to, haven't you? Mr. Giles said it was for you an' me both, it was our present, to share," she stressed the "our" solemnly, and Pip felt herself go pink. The fact that Skippy's mother watched her with sympathetic eyes only added to her confusion. People who were in love themselves were prone to insight where it affected others, and her secret was too precious, and too painful, to be bared.

"He must have known we were planning to go on the common this afternoon." She spoke hastily, trying to cover her embarrassment with speech. "We'll go well equipped." She turned away from the other woman's kindly smile, fighting for composure. "This is a beauty," she repeated, holding the kite up and away from her, testing it against the wind outside the kitchen door, feeling the resisting tug of its sail against her fingers even this near to the ground. She smiled back at the cheerful little bluebird painted on the canvas. "We'll soon have you on the wing," she promised with desperate gaiety.

"He mustn't fly away," Skippy joined in with her mood. "We'll have to hold on tight to the string."

"It sounds as if I'd better come along too, and hold on tight to you." Giles rounded the corner and took in the reception of his piece of workmanship with a satisfied look. "We can't have a bluebird carry you off." He swung Skippy on to his shoulder, but his eyes were on Pip's face. Waiting for her thanks?

"It's magnificent," she told him honestly. "You must have gone to a good deal of trouble." She didn't feel she could thank him for the present because she wasn't sure whether Skippy's explanation that it was for both of them might be just her usual enthusiasm for sharing her playthings, the reaction of an only child in a world of grown-ups, with no brother or sister with whom to own joint belongings.

"I guessed you'd like it." He still watched her, looking down from his much greater height, that seemed accentuated by the figure of the child on his shoulder, so that the shadow cast by the two of them fell long across her, cutting out the bright spring sunshine. Like loving him had done, she thought miserably, unable to meet his look because her feelings were plain in her own, so that she dropped her eyes to the suddenly blurred painting on the kite, her misted vision losing the outline of the bluebird and retaining only the stronger colour, the clear, dominant red of the rose it held in its beak. "Well, am I invited?" His voice was soft, gentle as when he spoke to Skippy or Betsy, and Pip thought he had spoken to the child. It was only when he repeated his question that she realised he had spoken to her.

"Invited? Yes – er – yes, of course," she stammered hurriedly. Now he'll think I don't want him to come – she realised her answer must sound lame, but her thoughts had been too intense for her to grasp his words. "I'll just go up and get my anorak." The wind was keen, but the edge of her poise was even keener, and she fled indoors, away from his gaze, away from the gentle smile of Skippy's mother, and heard as if in a dream the child's cry of "wait for me, I'm coming too!" as she took the stairs two at a time and buried her face in the depths of her wardrobe for fear Skippy's clear eyes should see what she hoped to hide from Giles. She pulled up the zip of her anorak with fingers that fumbled the simple task, and followed Skippy downstairs, one half of her longing to be with Giles, no matter what it cost, the other shrinking from the hurt of being with him, knowing that he would rather be with Stella.

"Stella told me you were going kite flying," he remarked as Skippy ran excitedly ahead of them, with Punch at her heels as usual. "It's years since I've flown a kite," he added wistfully, revealing for a moment the small boy that still lurks in every man under the adult shell.

"Let's see if you're out of practice." She handed him the object of their visit to the common, deliberately flippant, unable to think up any conversation since her wayward heart could tell her of only one thing she wanted to say to Giles, and that could not be spoken of. The fact that Stella had talked about her to Giles rankled in her mind. She didn't want Giles to feel sorry for her because she was staying on at the nursery over Easter. Her independent spirit rose at the thought and made her offhand in her manner towards him.

"This is flat enough for a run." He eyed the stretch of common ahead of them. "Let's see if we can get the kite in the air, then Skippy can hold the string." He gave her a keen look, hesitated, then evidently changed his mind about something and abruptly turned about and ran across the long stretch of close turf. Skippy and Punch chased gleefully after him, providing a noisy accompaniment to the sharp slap of the wind on the kite sail, and Pip was left on her own. A lark rose from somewhere nearby, trilling a tinny carol that sounded intermittently through the sharp gusts. She squinted against the sunshine until she could stand the brightness no longer, her gaze falling to the more sombre hue of the turf at her feet, starred with the bright faces of coltsfoot, and here and there new bracken fronds, unfurling like a child's blow flick at a party, crisp and green with new life from the feigned death of winter.

Would her feelings for Giles ever die? Pip wondered. Die and rise again to someone else's spring? She doubted if they would. Slowly she forced her feet to follow him, suddenly weary and unwilling to expose herself to further hurt, but unable to go home because she had promised Skippy's mother to keep her out until teatime, and besides, what reason could she give to Giles and the child? A family passed them in the distance, happily tossing a coloured ball between them. I suppose Giles and I look like a married couple to them, she thought, out with the child and the dog for the afternoon. How appearances could deceive! Her eyes traced the outline of their new kite, high now against the sunny sky, riding the air currents easily with its long tail of bows outstretched behind it, the painted bluebird carrying Giles' rose no longer visible at this distance, but remote and out of reach, as was the man who held the string, she thought, watching his sure fingers manipulate the canvas sail, controlling its flight so that it had perforce to stay a far distance from him, while yet the tie between them denied it the right to ride the sky as it willed – denied it the right to be free.

CHAPTER SIX

THEY made a silent party on the way back. Skippy was quiet out of sheer exhaustion, and Pip because she was lost in her own thoughts, hardly conscious that the sun had slid away and left the common to the cold evening wind, and the rapidly approaching dusk. Punch plodded behind the trio, at Giles' heels, for he carried Skippy, while Pip carried the kite. The six-year-old steadfastly refused to release her precious handful of primroses that they had found in a sheltered dell literally carpeted with the lowly little plants, so that they had to be careful where they trod, and ended up curled close together on the one small, grassy patch that for some reason was bare of blossoms, to eat the handful of toffees that Giles magically produced at just the right moment when they all needed a breather. Even Punch shared their feast, smacking his jaws as the toffee stuck to his teeth, his tail wagging an energetic accompaniment to their gay laughter, for surprisingly Pip found she could laugh along with the other two, loving the tiny paradise in which they found themselves, tucked away from the world so that there seemed to be only the three of them together – no, four, for Punch qualified; the shaggy little mongrel was part of their afternoon, and to his companions he seemed almost human.

It couldn't last, of course. The world was there, waiting to claim them, and with a sigh that betrayed his reluctance Giles heaved himself to his feet, reached down for Pip's hand and pulled her up beside him, smiling down into her flushed face with a look as carefree as if the proposed new road had never been thought of, and his beloved home was safe. But reality was waiting for him, too, once they had left the confines of their little dell, and set off to retrace their steps across the footpath towards home. As they came to the end of the rough gorse and ling, Giles turned and looked back across the common, briefly, bleakly upon the acres of unused ground, through which the new road would scarcely make any impression, so vast it seemed in comparison with his own smallholding.

"Why my land?" His voice was scarcely audible, as if he spoke more to himself than to her, but the bitterness in it was unmistakable, in his tone, in his face, that was darkly etched against the evening sky, its expression sombre as the gathering night clouds, and Pip's spirits dropped to match his own, so that each walked in their own thankless world, and their bright afternoon was a memory already, apart from them, something quickly forgotten even by the child, who slept now against the man's shoulder, her limp hand loosing her posy so that the delicate flowers dropped one by one and scattered in the breeze on to the inhospitable moor behind them, to fade and die before the morning came again.

Betsy's cheerful welcome came as a relief, but even the bright elm logs cracking in the grate, sawn up and neatly stacked by George and Sam from the stricken victim of that earlier gale, whose dying throes had so nearly claimed two human lives, could not melt the cold feeling inside her that refused to go away. Giles had taken them on to the common for the afternoon, and now he was free to seek company more to his liking, his sense of duty satisfied.

At least Betsy's daughter seemed happy, thought Pip, glad despite her own unhappiness that things were working out for the other woman. Evidently her walk with George that afternoon had had a happy conclusion.

"We'm getting married come the fall," she confided in a whisper as she roused Skippy, who was dropping off to sleep over the last remains of her tea. "Come on up to bed, now," she coaxed. "I'll tell you all about it tomorrow when you're awake enough to listen," she promised her small daughter, stemming her sleepy query. "I declare you look as sleepy as the lass here," she told Pip, forestalling Punch's efforts to follow his small playmate upstairs.

"I am," Pip confessed. "I think I'll go up myself and lie and read. It's all that fresh air," she yawned, deliberately playing up to the other woman's concern, wanting now to be alone so that she could live again the bright hours, hold them to her and treasure them for even a short while before time blurred their memory, as a miser turns over his treasures only to find with the passing of the years that failing eyesight diminishes the glitter of his precious hoard.

Giles left the nursery early the next morning. She heard his car start before she got up, and he did not return until fairly late in the evening, when he stopped outside the cottage door and left Stella to come in to the supper Betsy was keeping hot for her, while he took her suitcases to her flat. Pip heard them talking together in the hall and she knelt and stirred the fire, making as much noise as possible so that she should not hear what it was they said, and the clatter of the poker against the grate would warn them both that someone was in the sitting room.

"Oh, there you are." Stella wandered in while Pip was still kneeling on the rug, and she turned and looked up at her colleague, wondering where Stella thought she was likely to be. Despite the fact that it was still an official holiday, Pip had buried the daytime hours in work, striving by physical occupation to still her restless mind. From the look on her face Stella had found pleasanter means of whiling away the holiday hours, her smile was gay – no, that was the old Stella, that brittle gaiety that sat like a hard mask on her countenance, like an armour against the world. This went deeper; her smile, her whole look of happiness, as it had before she went away. The lasting kind, thought Pip dully, and wondered how soon Stella would be free to grasp her happiness and take her place by Giles' side.

"I couldn't stand living here then," thought Pip with desperate anguish, "not after they're married." It was bad enough now, with her love newly acknowledged; to remain and watch their happiness together would be a form of torture. She didn't know how long it would take for Stella to obtain a divorce. She had a vague idea that the procedure was usually a long one, but if it wasn't contested. . . . I'd like to see his special rose come into bloom, she thought wistfully, to see if it realised the dream he had painted on to the canvas, and to witness it win at the County Show. She flinched away from the fact that Giles intended to name it then. There was only one name he could give it, now, but like everything else in life she could not have it both ways. If she wanted the joy of seeing Giles' rose win, and she was convinced, loyally, that it would, she would have to pay the price of seeing him name it after Stella.

Beyond that first comment that she had enjoyed her holiday, Stella said no more, making no remark on where she had been or what she had done. Pip had no need to ask who she had been with, she could guess for herself, and the knowledge hurt. Stella's constant stream of escorts stopped, too. One came, hopefully, only to be turned away from the door of the flat, and he did not return. Stella seemed to withdraw into herself, even less communicative than usual, content with some inner happiness that Pip could not reach, and she declined to share. Once or twice she went out for a stroll in the grounds on her own, not asking or seeming to desire any other company, though when she returned each time she was with Giles.

It puzzled Pip that she still wore her wedding ring. It

always had made her wonder why, since Stella was estranged from her first husband – her only husband, thought Pip crossly; Stella and Giles were not married yet, but they soon would be, what did a few weeks or even months matter? Perhaps it was merely custom that made her keep the tooled platinum band round her finger. Pip's hands were bare of such ornaments, but several of her friends who habitually wore a ring said they felt lost without it. Soon Giles would put a fresh one on Stella's finger. She wondered if it would be another of platinum, or one of gold. She liked the gold wedding rings herself, the small, bright circlet of precious ore that seemed to symbolise her concept of all that marriage at its best should be, and more often than not was, if both partners were willing to work to make it so, for each union by its very nature must be a unique structure of loving crafts-manship, moulded by hands that have no plan to guide them, and no course by which to steer their future way except the instinct of two hearts to follow the same path to its end, as the flighting swallows yearly follow their migrant way, drawn by the irresistible pull of inner longing that cannot be satisfied until it reaches home.

The Shieldon Nurseries would be Stella's home soon, unless the planners had their way. For Giles' sake Pip hoped that his home would be spared, Stella had no use for old places, she had openly said so once, regarding the lovely old buildings as an obsolete relic from the past, better replaced by more modern and therefore more easily run flats, with all mod cons laid on and no trouble to the occupant. And no richness in living there, either, thought Pip, her gaze wandering through her workroom window to the mellow walls circled by bright borders, for Giles spared no expense to beautify his own gardens.

"We sell beauty to others," she heard him say once to a workman who questioned his instructions to put out some plants in Betsy's cottage garden that would have sold for a considerable sum from the selling section of the nursery, "so I don't see why we shouldn't enjoy it ourselves as well." Giles had his way, and Betsy her plants, and Pip wondered if the nursery had to go to make way for the road, would Stella manage to persuade him to live in a flat? It would be a sterile existence for him, but for his wife he would probably do it – and suffer as a result, she thought, returning to her work with an effort.

Despite her early preparation of the frames for her tableau, the days fled by in the busy life of the nursery and dragged Pip along with them, drawing her inexorably towards the time of the function at the Manor Hotel in a whirlwind of too few hours and too many jobs, so that she had to make a conscious effort to free herself from the routine in order that she might clothe the frames herself and personally supervise the rest of the arrangements. To Giles their contribution to the function was something special, and she was determined that for him she would make it extra special. At least he would have something to look back upon and remember her by – this function, and the display at the County Show which would come after, and be crowned by the naming of his rose.

She had plenty of material to choose from with which to colour her frames. The one of the girl child, with its wide crinoline and old-fashioned poke bonnet, lent itself to the plentiful supply of early double tulips, whose frilly petals gave the dress a realistically dainty look, lifted high enough at the front to show a peep of white pantaloons, in white tulip heads of the same kind. She repeated the white in the bonnet, giving it a rim of the pink and white to match the dress, and sorted out some wide pink ribbon from the nursery stores.

"I thought I'd tie this on as bonnet strings, and a length for the sash," she explained when Giles appeared and cast an interested eye on her efforts. "If we put a fan under the orchestra staging it will help to keep the flowers cool, and make the ribbons flutter at the same time, which will give an illusion of movement to the figures."

103

"It looks great." Giles bent to help her ease the completed frame forward, and adjust the prop at the back. "It was a fantastic idea."

Heavens, he's catching his adjectives from Stella, thought Pip disgustedly, and checked herself for being unfair. He really was enthusiastic, the function and its hoped-for outcome meant a lot to him.

"Where are you going to keep this?" Giles indicated the completed frame. "You won't start setting it up in the hotel until tomorrow?"

"No, the less time the flowers spend in the hotel the better." Pip was adamant. "I'll keep them all in the cold room until then," she decided. "I'm going to start on the boy's figure now, then the shield," she ticked off the jobs, drawing a line across the list pinned to the wall next to the painting, which she carefully refrained from marking in deference to her promise to Skippy.

"You're methodical as well," drawled Giles, with a laugh in his voice that brought her round to face him, on the defensive, sensing that he was poking fun at her and not sure why.

"As well as what?" She didn't want to ask the question, but it came before she could stop it, and the smile deepened in his eyes, that warmed as only brown eyes can, losing for a moment that look of bleak remoteness that seemed to be their only expression when Pip first came to the nursery. It's marvellous what love can do, she thought, even to someone so seemingly self-sufficient as Giles. She hoped that Stella would use her power over him gently, so that the smile remained in their depths and did not fade, as the thought of the potential fate of his home could make it fade so quickly.

"Ah, that would be telling!" He assumed a mysterious expression, and took the other end of the completed figure, helping her through the workroom door and across the wide gravelled path to the cold room opposite.

"Brrr! The flowers are welcome to their stay in there,"

Giles shivered as he shut the door firmly behind him.

"I'll bring them out tomorrow morning," Pip assured him, desperately holding on to practicalities, not daring to meet his look when he smiled at her like that. "I'll stand them outside first thing and spray them well, it'll give them time to drain free of surplus water before we take them into the Manor. We can't have a water festival on our hands, even if the reason for it all is a swimming pool for the hospital," she quipped, and wondered where she found the strength to joke. "Now for the figure of the boy. . . ."

"I'd like to stay and watch – may I? I won't if I'm in the way." He turned towards the door as he saw Pip hesitate.

"No, don't go!" She put out a quick hand to stop him. "I was thinking, that's all," she said lamely. "Stay if you're interested," she managed casually, turning away from him to pick up the other frame, pretending an indifference she could never feel again towards the man behind her. Her hands trembled as she reached for the basket of scarlet tulips beside her, so that she fumbled the first two, and cut the stems too short, had difficulty in fixing them until Giles reached out to help her. "I can manage." She didn't want him to help her, daren't let him come too close, and he desisted and sat back again on the edge of her workbench under the window, away from where she worked in the centre of the floor in front of the painting on the wall so that she could follow the guiding colours as she blocked in with her living material the scarlet trousers and butter-yellow shirt, and gay scarlet beret. Her fingers worked swiftly, placing the flower heads so that the frame was covered in brilliant colour, and the completed figure of the boy looked as if it had stepped straight from the painting on the wall and come to life under her hands.

"You're an artist," Giles said softly, when she had done, and stepped back beside him to criticise the result.

"Not in your class," Pip denied. "I can't hang these in a frame on the wall, like your painting of the rose. That's. . . ."

"A dream," he responded quietly. "I told you. . . ."

"Do you always paint your dreams?" Stella's dark beauty would make any artist pause and reach for a brush.

"Sometimes they aren't tangible enough." He refused to be drawn, and Pip bent and silently lifted her end of the completed figure, taking it to join its fellow in the cold room. "There's only the shield now."

"That's a good size." Giles eyed the frame consideringly.

"I know, but it's not so complicated as the other two," Pip returned, settling herself back on to her stool. "The background is simple, it's all white, and these small chrysanths will be ideal for making a solid cushion. I'm using yellow roses for the rosebud in the centre of the shield," she told him, talking at random to keep her thoughts at bay.

"What about the outline?"

"Roses again, those very dark red ones. George gave me a basketful just now." She uncovered her supply for his appraisal, and he squatted down on the floor beside the box and reached for her clippers.

"The stalks of those are fairly tough, tell me how long you want them and I'll clip them for you."

"I'd be grateful." She spoke the truth, the ends of her fingers were beginning to feel sore. She had been working with scarcely a break for hours, determined to do the job herself, and driven by the need to have it completed by nightfall so that the setting up might proceed without a check the next morning, since she had purloined a number of George's staff to help her with the fetching and carrying, and she did not want to leave him short-handed for any longer than she had to.

"That will do fine," as Giles held up a rose clipped to

the required length, and he nodded silently, anticipating her movements, and working alongside her companionably as she had worked with him when he made the frames.

"That's enough, I think." Pip shook her head, refusing his last offered bloom. "I wish I hadn't let you cut it," she looked at the shortened stalk regretfully, "it could have gone with the others into the selling section. There's still enough left for a small bunch."

"In my experience red roses usually sell in ones, as specials," Giles smiled significantly, and Pip blushed. She knew – everyone in the nursery knew and joked about it – that the selling section had enjoyed a bumper turnover on St. Valentine's Day, most of it from red roses, sold singly in the attractive gift boxes the nursery provided. "This one needn't be wasted." His voice and face were expressionless, his fingers busy fashioning a delicate lace of green fern about the deep red bud. "Tuck it in your buttonhole," he bade her, and held it out towards her with an inscrutable look.

The fern felt soft against her fingers, and spread out in an arc around the perfect bud, so that it was held upright when Pip placed it in the narrow cut glass vase that Betsy had provided for her when she first arrived, and discovered that she enjoyed having cut blooms in her room.

She took it out and pinned it to the shoulder of her sweater the next morning, reluctant to leave it behind her when she started the sizeable task of setting up her display at the Manor Hotel. The completed frames, removed from the cold room and thoroughly sprayed so that the thick, padded base of them would remain damp and keep the flowers fresh in the warm atmosphere that would prevail during the hours of the function, drew gasps of admiration from her small band of helpers who fetched and carried with a cheerful willingness that soon had the large van load of primulas, pansies, violas and miniature tulips massed in a vivid, multi-coloured carpet in front of the orchestra dais in the ballroom. The figures of the dancing children were raised above them on moss-covered blocks, to make it appear as if they were skipping across the surface of the blossoms, their upraised hands joined by a string of flower heads that made a most effective daisy chain, repeated round the walls of the ballroom, and again in the dining room, linking the carefully made nursery shield that sat behind the top table with the simple floral arrangements placed high on the windowsills.

The tables themselves had to be left until the last, and Pip was beginning to feel distinctly weary by the time the alternate ellipse-shaped blocks of miniature roses and pansies had been arranged to her satisfaction, and there was nothing more to do except go home and change into her evening dress in time to return to the hotel. She left the van parked outside the cottage door, as soon as the dinner at the hotel was over and the diners dispersed, she intended to strip the tables of their decorations and take them straight to the hospital, where a tiny rose tree or a tub of bright pansies would appear on each child's bedside locker the next morning when they awoke.

She felt glad Giles had suggested she go to the hotel in evening dress. She would not feel as conspicuous among the dancers as if she was in working gear, however tidy. Caution made her stock the back of the van with a small supply of the potted plants that made up the "carpet" in the ballroom, so that she could unobtrusively replace any that showed signs of wilting in the warmth, and she wondered, not for the first time, if she ought to have used pansies and violas for fear of this very reaction, but pansies were children's flowers, as were the primulas in a way, and she had geared her effect for simplicity, which would have been lost had she used the hardier but more sophisticated chrysanthemum blooms, of which the nursery still had pots aplenty.

"Thank goodness that's done!" She collapsed into a

chair in the sitting room at the cottage. "I shall have an hour's sit down while they're all at dinner, and I can grab a snack then," she told Betsy, replying to her landlady's frowning comment that she looked more ready for an early night than a dance.

"You've been on the go since six," the grey-haired little woman said severely.

"I don't expect to be very late back," Pip assured her. "Once I've delivered the flowers to the hospital I can go back to the hotel and do a final round of the set-up. Any pots that are going to wilt will show signs of it by then, and once they're checked over I can come straight home." She didn't want to stay and watch Giles dancing with his partner, didn't want him to feel obliged, out of pure politeness, to ask her to dance. I wonder who he's going with? she thought. Stella? But Stella would have found some way to let her know, if only out of spite. She had remained silent about her activities at Easter, it was true, but if she was attending the function at the Manor she couldn't hope to keep that to herself; for one thing she would have to change into evening dress, and she was still in slacks and sweater, and intended to remain in them for the rest of the evening from the look of her elegantly comfortable position, lounging full-length in her chair and taking her time over her cigarette and coffee. "I'll be back in time for supper, so save me some coffee," she reminded her companion.

"Pleasure," drawled the dark-haired girl, "but I thought – didn't Giles . . . ? Oh well, we'll keep some hot for you," she promised with a shrug and a puzzled look in Pip's direction that cast doubts about her wanting the coffee even if it was saved for her.

"She must think I'm partnering Giles," thought Pip with wry amusement, but there was no time to explain now. She brushed her hair up into a fluffy ball round her head, the ends still damp from her bath, and stepped into her long dress, tugging the zip to the top with a practised wriggle. She looked at her red rosebud, which was back in its vase again, but opening now, half way to fading, she thought regretfully. She'd press it, she decided, stroking the unfurling petals with gentle fingers. If she wore it again it would fade beyond recall, and remembering Giles' remark about the usual method of selling red roses she shrank from pinning it to her dress for fear he should tease her about its significance, tease her probably in front of his partner, and that she felt she could not bear. Why wasn't he partnering Stella? she wondered, and found her answer easily enough when she remembered how long the function had been arranged. Doubtless Giles had promised to take one of his county friends before he and Stella had become close, and he was not the sort of man to break a promise. Before the elm tree crashed, Giles and Stella hadn't seemed to take a lot of notice of one another; it was only since then that Stella had deliberately set out to attract his attention, with every appearance of success.

Pip slipped her long evening cloak over her dress, the warm folds of velvet welcome in the evening chill. Her slippers were flat-heeled and would not hinder her from driving. She checked in her evening bag to make sure she had got her key before she latched the front door behind her and stopped abruptly on the gravelled path outside the cottage at the sight of Giles in full evening dress busily transferring her spare pot plants from the back of the van into the opened boot of his own car.

"What's the matter? Has a tyre gone?" There was dismay in her voice. Of all nights for the van to fail her, it had to choose this one! she thought with exasperation. Giles ducked from inside the open rear doors and emerged with a box of pansies in each hand.

"Sam told me you intended taking the van yourself." His scowl was black. "Where's George?" he demanded.

"Gone home, of course. Why?" Pip was puzzled by his curt tone. It was long past nursery working hours, and since she always drove her own van she couldn't see why she had to ask George to drive it for her this evening. It was not the first time she had had to do similar work after hours, and she did not suppose it would be the last.

"I didn't invite you to a dance and expect you to drive there on your own in the works van." His voice was grim. "Unless you want to, of course?" He frowned down at her severely, and spoiled the effect by straightening up to his full height and cracking his head on the raised boot lid of his car.

"Damn!" His scowl grew even blacker, and Pip raised her fingers to her lips, stifling a sudden, overpowering desire to giggle. She mustn't laugh, not at Giles, and not now. Thank goodness it was dusk, and she was in the shadow of the van doors, so that he could not see her expression.

"Have you hurt yourself?" Her voice quavered, but he might think that was anxiety.

"No," he answered her shortly, fixing the boxes of flowers so that they would not slide about in the boot, and slamming the lid shut with unnecessary force. "Well?" he demanded, but his tone was milder, his sudden flash of temper evaporated once the flowers were out of sight. "Do you really want to drive yourself? I don't make a habit of having near misses with sports cars," he added feelingly, referring to the last time he had given her a lift as far as the Manor Hotel.

He must think I'm nervous of his driving, thought Pip, a wave of relief coursing through her. Dislike of being a passenger was a common enough phobia among drivers.

"I thought I was going to the Manor tonight to work," she said, as he waited with every sign of impatience for her to answer.

"You are – we both are," he assured her, "but we might as well enjoy the evening as well, at least we can see how our efforts are received," he told her crisply, and her spirits dropped. It would have been nice if he had asked her to go with him because he wanted her company, instead of as a reward for her hard work, she thought mournfully. She herself had rewarded Skippy with a toffee bar for her help, which was suitable thanks for a six-year-old, but hardly satisfying to be rewarded in such a manner when you are grown-up – and in love, her heart reminded her, adding depression to the weariness that she thought she had shed with her bath and change of clothes earlier. And he had not really asked her anyhow, she told herself with ruthless honesty, he had simply instructed her to make herself available for the function, and suggested it would be as well if she wore evening dress. How was she supposed to know from such an instruction that she was expected to remain for the dinner and dance? she thought crossly. She wasn't clairvoyant!

"In that case, I'll accept a lift." Vexation helped her to be flippant, and in the fading light she saw his lips quirk upwards in a quick grin.

"Touché!" He opened the car door, his good humour restored, and tucked her safely into the passenger seat, bending to make sure the long folds of her dress and cloak were stowed clear of the door. "I'll go and put the van away before we set off." He strode away, and faintly through the car windows Pip heard him whistling. It sounded like the first bars of the Skaters' Waltz, and unconsciously she started to hum it as well, losing herself in the catchy rhythm so that she jumped when he appeared without warning beside her.

"Catching, isn't it?" he smiled. "Maybe they'll play it for us," he hoped as he escorted her up the entrance steps of the Manor, brilliantly lit and decked with carnival bunting for the occasion. "Hello there!" He responded to the greetings that met him on every side, turning towards a small knot of people whom Pip had seen before at the nursery, his hand on her arm, drawing her along beside him to be among his friends.

"Pip, you've already met. . . ." Her hand was caught and shaken, and she found herself responding to the unselfconscious friendliness that accepted her as one of themselves, not, she sensed, simply because she was Giles' partner, but because her companions liked her for herself, and were glad that she had come among them. Briefly, on the journey in, she had panicked about her dress. Was it too plain? Too bright? Should she have borrowed one from Stella? Now she could relax; her dress drew more than one murmured comment that was a compliment to her taste as well as to the beauty of her gown.

"You're responsible for bringing the loveliest decoration here tonight, Giles," an elderly man on Pip's right bowed in a courtly manner across the expanse of white damask and gleaming silver, and his tone and the admiring look he cast in her direction were alike significant with double meaning.

"I agree," Giles smiled back, "and the flowers themselves were Pip's idea," he answered the other's congratulatory comment. Giles was generous as well as truthful.

"You helped," Pip protested, her colour rising, but pleased despite her disclaimer. All the work she had put in had been more than worth while, she thought. The proprietor of the hotel had been so impressed himself by the unusual display that he had diverted the route to the dining room through part of the ballroom so that the diners might have a preview of the colourful tableau set beneath the orchestra dais, and the effect was flattering in the extreme. Congratulations were showered on Giles from all sides by people who could not have known that Pip was responsible, since she was a stranger to them, and he made no attempt to hide his pleasure in their comments. For his sake, Pip felt glad. At least she would have given him something worthwhile to remember, this and the display in June of which his unnamed rose would be the centrepiece. She must start planning that as well, now. She had got until June, but June was not very far away, a matter of a few short weeks that, if all went well, would see the culmination of Giles' ambition so far as his rose was concerned, and the end of her stay at the nursery.

"Oh, I did the labouring," Giles laughed. "Pip insisted on doing the figures herself."

"I hope he was worthy of his hire." The Lord Mayor's teasing voice brought her back to her surroundings, and he looked at her with a twinkle in his eye. Despite his formidable-looking chain of office, Pip had discovered him to be an amiable countryman of likeable disposition, and his wife a charming little woman to whom she took an immediate liking. She was glad they were placed next to them at the top table. Most of Giles' personal friends seemed to be ranged along their table, she realised, glancing across their array of near neighbours.

"My orchid came from your nursery." The Lady Mayoress leaned across her husband to show off the flower pinned to the shoulder of her gown. "Isn't it gorgeous? I like the simpler flowers better, really," she confessed, with a disarming smile, "but for an occasion like this – well, orchids are so special, aren't they? Giles should have given you one to wear," she scolded him gently. "After doing such wonderful work," she waved an expressive hand at the floral shield behind their table. "Don't you agree?" she appealed to her husband.

"You're not even wearing a flower," the Lord Mayor observed kindly. "Don't tell me you're tired of them?" he smiled.

"She just hasn't had time to pin it on. Allow me." Giles picked up a golden rosebud that lay beside Pip's place card on the table, and which she hadn't noticed until now. "It isn't an orchid, I know," he acknowledged the Mayoress's smiling interest as he turned Pip to face him, and clipped the dainty rose to her dress.

"A gold rosebud – why, that's like the one on your

shield, Giles," their distinguished neighbour exclaimed.

"That's right." Giles patted his handiwork into place with professional skill. "It's the nursery badge," he remarked complacently.

CHAPTER SEVEN

SHE wished he had not put it like that. If he had given her the flower as a casual gift she would not have minded so much, a small pleasantry to mark the evening, with no significance to it, as he had given her the red rose, the odd flower left from the work they had shared, and fashioned into a quick buttonhole with a piece of fern, rather than waste it. But – "It's the nursery badge." The indifferent comment took all the pleasure from her rose, from the excellent dinner in front of her, and the gay company of which they were a part, and to which she now found it so difficult to respond. The brilliance of the glittering chandeliers, and the vivid rainbow of evening dresses seemed dulled, and she herself felt labelled. Ticketed, she thought furiously, marked with an identifying stamp as if she was part of the nursery equipment, just as the flower holders and the frames and all the paraphernalia of the display in the ballroom were a part of the nursery equipment, to be removed from the hotel once the dance was over, taken away and stored out of sight until it was needed for some future use.

Pip bent mutinous eyes on her plate, scarcely aware of what it contained, only aware that she didn't want whatever it was, and wished she could be back safely in Betsy's warm cottage, to run up to the privacy of her own room and shut herself away from the lights, and the flashing bulbs of cameras carried by reporters from several of the local newspapers, who were laughingly encouraged by the diners, for the newsmen had done much through their own particular medium to raise funds for the swimming pool. Most of all she longed to hide herself away from the interested eyes of her fellow guests, for she had been conscious of their glances, and the interest they held, from the moment she walked up the hotel steps at Giles' side. There was carefully veiled curiosity in the greetings of the people to whom she was introduced, and speculation, veiled by good manners, but evident nevertheless, at least to her. Giles seemed unconscious of anything but the surface friendliness, cheerfully drawing Pip into any conversation of which he became a part, deferring to her opinion, treating her as if she was indeed his invited partner instead of just an employee, except for that one brief, unthinking remark "It's the nursery badge". And after the meal was over, and the speeches and the toasting done, he punctiliously introduced her to those to whom he stopped to speak, and there were many, for he was evidently popular, and small groups of people on all sides detained him on one pretext or another, until Pip's hand ached with shaking those of others, and her mind reeled with names that she could not hope to remember, there were so many.

"Let's have a picture, Mr. Shieldon." One of the reporters stepped in front of them, laughingly blocking their way, and levelling his camera. Pip noticed with amusement that her earlier acquaintance from the *Echo* kept well in the background; evidently Giles had spoken his mind about the article on the elm tree and the effect of his words still persisted. "One of you and your young lady," the man with the camera begged. He was young and brash, with none of the tact evinced by Giles' personal friends, and Pip felt her colour rise, and glanced up at her partner uncertainly, but with unshakeable good humour Giles put his arm about her shoulder and turned her to face the lens.

"Smile," he bade her, smiling down at her himself as the bulb flashed and caught her by surprise.

"That'll be the scoop of the week," she told him ruefully. "I'll probably come out with my eyes closed."

"In that case we'll sue him if he prints it," Giles assured her, patting the young reporter's shoulder in a friendly fashion as he turned towards the exit, intent on getting his story in the morning edition of his paper. "Never mind his picture," he went on, tightening his arm about her, that had somehow slipped from her shoulder and was now about her waist. "Let's enjoy the dance." The orchestra had struck up a tango, and without waiting for her to answer Giles swung her on to the floor, not asking if she could tango, or even if she wanted to, she thought, her earlier rebellion coming back. He had pinned his badge to her dress, and seemed to feel it gave him the right to dictate her every move, she thought angrily, but somehow, in spite of her feelings, and her urge to pull away, his arms impelled her to follow his steps, holding her closely against him so that they moved as one to the insistent throb of music that had been born of more exotic lands, under hot southern skies, for a people whose fiery blood abandoned them to dances that were a vivid mime of their colourful lives, drawn by the wild strings of gipsy violins under velvet, starlit skies.

"He's a wonderful dancer." The realisation brought surprise that the aloof, reserved man she knew should be able to give himself to the music with the relaxed grace that stamped him as master of the art. No mean performer herself, the joy of dancing with a partner of such prowess dissolved Pip's annoyance, and she swung into the dance with Giles, enjoyment evident in her every move, careless of the vividly coloured underpleating of her skirt that opened like bright sunrays about her lissom figure, unaware of the strange hush that descended on the ballroom, and the cessation of movement by the other dancers until the music died away, and she realised with quick confusion that she and Giles had been the only couple to finish the tango. The other guests had quietly formed a circle about them, and a ripple of applause greeted their performance as they quit the floor together. Shyness gripped her, and she longed to hurry, to lose herself among the crowd, sure that Stella would have coped with the situation with far more poise, but Giles' hand through her arm kept her by his side.

"You two ought to go in for competition dancing," the Lord Mayor congratulated them.

"Pip's a wonderful dancer, isn't she?" Giles generously turned the praise on to his partner.

"You must save me a dance." "And me," several voices added in unison, hopefully, and Giles shook his head in mock severity.

"Later," he told them. "We've promised to take the table decorations up to the hospital for the children," he explained to their disappointed protests. "We thought it would be nice for them to wake up and find a tub of flowers on their lockers tomorrow morning."

"What a wonderful idea!" the Mayoress beamed her approval.

"You stay and dance. I can manage the flowers once they're in the van – oh. . . ." Pip remembered she hadn't got the van with her.

"Certainly not, we'll go together. I won't be denied the pleasure," retorted Giles firmly, with an unfathomable look in her direction which she didn't see because she turned away, unwilling to let him see her face for fear it might reflect her feelings. It would have been nice if the pleasure he would not forgo was her company, she thought forlornly, and made her excuses to the kindly expressions of disappointment from their companions with a smile that only stern self-discipline kept in place.

Waiters were busy stripping the tables when they returned to the dining room together, and they both paused at the door, struck by the sense of disillusionment everyone feels when returning to the scene of some festivity once it is over. All but three of the main lights had been extinguished, they gave adequate illumination for the hotel staff to do their work, but the effect was one of overall gloom, in which the high-swung chandeliers were left suspended in semi-darkness, like the ghosts of sailing ships riding the mists of time past, only the lower crystals of the earlier glittering tiers catching an occasional gleam from the lamps that struck a momentary spark of colour off them to pierce the deserted, silent hall that had so recently teemed with gay, chattering life and moving colour.

"It feels a bit like . . . after Christmas. . . ." Pip was inarticulate, but Giles nodded as if he understood.

"I know." His voice was subdued, his hand momentarily tightening its grip on her arm.

"Mr. Shieldon?" One of the waiters looked round at the sound of their voices, and approached soft-footed across the carpet.

"We've come to collect the table decorations," Giles explained their presence. "We're taking them to the hospital for the children."

"Yes, I know, sir. It's a grand idea," the man approved. "We'll help you load up," he offered, and Giles hesitated.

"We were going to manage between us," he indicated Pip beside him, "but if you're sure you've got the time? It would be a lot quicker," he accepted gratefully.

"You go and run your car round to the front and open the boot, sir," the man suggested, "and we'll carry the pots of flowers. With you in evening clothes, and all," he ignored his own similar, working attire, "and it would be a pity to risk marking your young lady's evening dress," he added gallantly.

He's as bad as the reporter, thought Pip sourly; the newspaper man had called her Giles' young lady. A natural enough mistake, but – heavens! A sudden thought struck her. What if the reporter put his expression into print? She could just imagine Stella's reaction. And what would Giles feel? she wondered. Particularly if his friends pulled his leg about it. He had been amiability itself to the reporter, but that was in the middle of the guests at the function. Tomorrow, in the cold light of day, he might not be quite so sweet-tempered, she realised, and hoped her work would take her to the other side of the nursery for a day or two until the aftermath had blown over. Her own feelings were too fragile to stand that kind of teasing, she decided, determined if her fears were justified to snub the first attempt at misplaced humour.

"I'll go and fetch the car." Giles left her with a murmured apology, and she stood in the shadowed dining room watching the four waiters carefully lift the individual pots of flowers from their mossy bed on the tables, ruthlessly using the best hotel trays to hold them, and the dinner wagons that somehow appeared from the nether regions of the dining room to transport them to the front entrance.

"You've certainly got yourself well organised," laughed Giles, approving their quick turnabout.

"We'd got it planned, sir. When we knew what you intended to do with them, we thought the sooner they were out of the hot dining room the better." The head waiter looked gratified. "We'd have liked to come along and help you give them out, but there's supper to serve yet." He looked his disappointment, revealing a warm, human countenance in place of the imperturbable Jeeves-like shell that had awed Pip at the dinner table.

"Have you got any children?" Giles stopped half way down the steps, his look thoughtful.

"We've all got two each except for Tom here, he's only got one – yet," the head waiter grinned. "That's why we're all so keen to help, I expect," he backed away hastily from his good deed.

"Then keep that trayload for your own youngsters." Giles counted the contents quickly. "There's eight pots there, that's one each for them, and one to spare," he smiled at the waiter called Tom, who went brick red and shuffled uncomfortably, but looked pleased nevertheless. "No, don't worry, there's plenty to spare, we made sure of that. Enough to decorate the playroom at the hospital as well," he assured the demurring man. "We'll be taking the rest of the decorations from the ballroom tomorrow morning, they'll like the figures of the children done in flowers, I expect." He waved aside their thanks and bent to open the car door for Pip. "There's not a lot of room left for you and me, but we'll manage." He tucked her in and gave an amused glance at the rear compartment. "The boot's full as well, there isn't an inch to spare," he told her in a satisfied tone. He raised a friendly hand to the waiters on the steps, who cheerfully waved back as he set the car in motion and steered carefully down the drive to the main road. "We'll go slowly, I don't want to disturb the pots any more than I can help." He turned the bonnet on to the main road heading away from the town. The hospital was some distance away, Pip knew; she had passed it once or twice on her journeys to various assignments, but had never been inside the grounds, which looked fairly extensive from the road.

"It was built by one of the nouveau riche after the first world war, on the profits of misery, I suspect," Giles answered her question. "As a private house it was a pretentious place, but as a hospital it's ideal, well placed, and surprisingly well laid out inside. It wasn't too expensive to convert."

So the conversion from house to hospital had been done within Giles' memory, at least.

"Who converted it, the National Health?"

"No, they took it over later, of course, and it's one of the best of its kind in the country now, but the original place was set up at the expense of – well – local families, mostly," he hedged, his withdrawal telling Pip more clearly than if he had expressed it that his own family had been one, perhaps the major one, of the number. No wonder he had such an interest in the place, she thought, respecting his reserve.

"Well now, you didn't stay to enjoy the dancing for long." The Matron received them warmly, both her hands held out towards Giles, who bent and kissed her affectionately. This was another side of the man she knew nothing about, Pip realised, and wondered if many people outside his own immediate circle did. "I knew him when he was little enough to spank," the white-haired woman twinkled at Pip, reaching out and grasping her hands in turn, and planting a motherly kiss on her cheek. "Come along in, the night's cold. Though I don't expect you two young ones feel it," she smiled mischievously, but her manner was so kindly that this time Pip didn't even feel uncomfortable.

She just wished there were grounds for the Matron's assumptions. What would be the good lady's reaction to Stella? she wondered, for when she and Giles were married she had no doubt that at some time he would bring her here too. That is, if Stella would come. Or would this be another of those things that she declared were "not her cup of tea"? Pip shook her head, trying to check the trend of her thoughts, grateful for the warmth of the cosy study into which they had been shown, and the real cup of tea that was thrust into her hand in a "won't take no for an answer" manner, so that surprisingly she found herself enjoying it despite her recent meal, relaxing in the quiet room away from the noise and bustle of the crowd they had just left. She had, as Betsy said, been up since before six o'clock, and the hectic day behind her was beginning to tell. She lay back in the easy chair pulled close to the warm fire and relaxed, ready enough to leave the talking to the others. They seemed to have a lot of news to exchange, she thought sleepily. The soft hum of their voices grew fainter, and she roused with a start as she felt her cup taken from her hand.

"Giles, you're working this child much too hard." Two

shrewd eyes took in the faint smudges under Pip's own, with a penetrating, all-embracing glance that Pip feared might glean more than surface information, so that she sat up hurriedly.

"It's the warmth of your fire," she apologised for her lapse.

"We shan't be late going home," Giles reassured their hostess. "We'll have to go back to the Manor, but one more dance should be enough, and then we can decently take our leave if we want to." His tone said he would leave the decision to Pip.

"Come and see the bairns." The matron bustled towards the door. "I've left an old trolley in the hall for the flowers," she told them, and Giles' eyes widened as he saw the long, wheeled stretcher standing ready for them.

"You're as well organised as the waiters at the Manor," he congratulated her. "It's just the job."

"Oh, we northerners know what we're talking about," the matron twinkled a conspiratorial look in Pip's direction, and surprised a chuckle out of her that brought a quick light to the man's eyes.

"You two are clanning up on me," he complained. "You talk a language of your own. Pip calls our stream a burn," he mimicked her soft accent teasingly, struggling out of the car door with his arms full of flower pots. "Form a chain and help me with these," he begged them, passing his load on to Pip. It was a good suggestion, and in no time the car was empty and the trolley loaded. "Now for the wards. Lead on, Mac," he bade the matron disrespectfully, and with Giles and Pip providing the pushing power, and their guide steering the front of the long trolley in the right direction, they headed along a corridor that smelt faintly of polish. The matron took them through a set of double doors at the end that led into a dimly lit room, the rubber wheels of the trolley making scarcely a sound on the smooth floor so they had no fear of waking the occupants. A woman in nurse's uniform rose from a desk in the corner and smiled a greeting.

"They're all fast asleep except Jimmy," she reported in a low voice, and the matron nodded, satisfied.

"Right, you take that side, Giles. Pip and I will do this one." She was evidently enjoying her task, and Pip joined in eagerly, tiptoeing between each cot and leaving a miniature rose bush on one locker, and a tub of pansies on the next, alternately, so as to forestall any young arguments the next morning as to who owned which. If they had the energy to argue, Pip thought compassionately, looking down at the small, sleeping forms in the high-sided cots.

"They'll argue," the matron assured her. "It's surprising the amount of energy they can generate," she said feelingly. "That swimming pool will help a lot," she divined Pip's thoughts accurately. "Most of these little ones will be on their feet and back at home more quickly because of it." Pip nodded dumbly, suddenly unable to speak, humbled by the good fortune of her own sound limbs that made her feel suddenly, clumsily strong.

"Where's Giles?" She realised her companion had disappeared, and the trolley was empty of flower pots.

"He's on the veranda." The night nurse appeared silently at their side and indicated a door leading outside. "He's talking to Jimmy."

The one who wasn't asleep. Pip glanced at the matron, wondering if Giles was in for a scolding, but she merely smiled and beckoned Pip to follow him through the door.

"Go and join him," she suggested, "and when you're ready bring him back to my study. I'll take the trolley back out of the way."

She trundled their empty transport back the way they had come, and at a nod from the nurse Pip slipped through the doors and on to the open veranda that held four beds. Giles was sat on a stool beside one, holding its occupant's small hand, and from the sound of it telling him a bedtime story, Pip surmised accurately.

". . . happily ever after," she heard him come to that most satisfactory of all conclusions, and he bent and tucked the bedclothes gently about the now drowsy child. Giles could be wonderfully gentle, she had noticed before, when he was with Skippy or Betsy, or when he was handling his beloved flowers.

"Will my flowers be here in the morning?" a small voice piped up from the pillow.

"They'll be here," he promised, turning the tub of bright yellow pansies on the locker so that they could be easily seen from the bed. "Now go off to sleep. 'Night, Jimmy!"

A contented sigh was his only answer, and Giles crept away, leaving the field clear for the smiling nurse to do her rounds in peace. Pip noticed that he had thoughtfully left a small rose bush on her desk, too, as well as one on the matron's.

"Tell me how your special rose is getting on," his elderly friend bade him when they returned to her study.

"It's coming along well." Giles' look was eager, his hobbyhorse was being patted and the matron smiled at his enthusiastic response. "The bushes are already shooting well."

"Aren't they a bit early?" she murmured doubtfully. "Mine are only just beginning to look as if they intend to live. What if there's a frost?"

"Frost is hardly likely this late in the year," Giles retorted. "We're long past Easter, and besides, the bushes are all in the walled garden. That's what makes them so forward. The walls create a micro-climate that's warmer than the open garden," he explained.

"There won't be a frost again this year," Pip stated positively. "George – he's the foreman at the nursery," she identified him to her hostess, "George had the dahlias bedded out this week, and he's never wrong about the weather," she claimed.

"I hope your faith is justified." Giles cocked an eye at the clear, moonlit sky on their way back to the hotel. "It feels colder."

"That's only because we've come out of a warm room, I expect," Pip answered. "That fire in the study was a beauty," she remembered appreciatively.

"Mac loves a good roast, as she calls it," Giles laughed. "She ought to know better than to live in that fug, in her profession. By the way," he sidetracked, "do you still feel tired? We can go straight home if you'd rather," he offered considerately.

"Goodness, no! I'm wide awake now. It was the fug, as you called it," she assured him, reluctant to be responsible for taking him away from his friends, and glad as he guided her on to the dance floor for the second time that evening that she had elected to return with him. The firm feel of his arm encircling her, and her hand in his warm clasp, made her feel safe, she thought, wishing she could stay within the circle of his arm for ever. Giles had that quiet strength that would shelter the woman he loved, so that from the safety of that shelter she could face any storms that might blow, secure in the knowledge that whatever else might change, his love would endure, for instinctively Pip knew that the man who held her would regard the marriage vows as sacred, and expect his partner to do the same.

"I suppose you'll go into hibernation again until the County Show," the Mayoress accused him playfully. "You really ought to bully him into going out more often," she told Pip. "He usually only comes to these functions on sufferance, and then he has to be dragged along," she scolded.

"Tonight I'm really enjoying myself," Giles smiled at her, relieving Pip of the necessity of answering. She felt mightily embarrassed, wishing that she could explain her position. Evidently Giles had not thought it necessary and her new-found friends probably thought that her check of the floral display on their return to the hotel was nothing more than an over-developed sense of responsibility, she thought ruefully. But at least she could believe that Giles spoke the truth, for his pleasure in the evening was obvious, and she guessed that most of it stemmed from his sojourn at the hospital, and that brief, quiet moment telling a bedtime story to a sick child. He would probably have enjoyed the dinner and dance part of the evening more if he had been with Stella, she surmised, then it would have been pure pleasure and not a continuation of work, but his determination to let nothing stand in the way of a swimming pool for the hospital had evidently breached his normal reserve. She had never known him unbend so completely.

"You'll be showing at the County, won't you, Giles?" The Mayor turned to him, interested in his answer.

"Of course he will. He promised to name his rose there," the dignitary's wife butted in. "Won't you let us in on the secret, Giles? Or have we got to wait until the Show to find out?" she pouted.

"I've got to wait until nearly the Show to find out for myself," he retorted. "Remember the bushes have to bloom yet, and if they're up to standard – only if, mind you – then the best buds will be put in the Show as the centre of our display."

"Will you be responsible for the rest of the display, Pip?" The Mayor smiled at her in a kindly manner. "If it's anywhere near the success of this one you're bound to win first prize," he told her loyally.

"I – er – " Pip's eyes sought Giles' face for her answer. Was she to be in charge of the display for the County Show? She expected to, but so much hung on this particular display, the launching of his rose in particular, that he might decide to take over himself.

"Yes, Pip will be in charge. It's getting a habit," he answered, with an oblique look in her direction so that

Pip didn't know whether he was joking or serious, and if he was serious, whether he was being sarcastic or not. Well, at least he can't complain about the decorations tonight, she thought wrathfully; they had brought a delighted response from guests and hotel staff alike, and a whole ballroom full of people couldn't be wrong. "That's why you won't be seeing much of me until then," her escort told his friends imperturbably. "The Show's in a few weeks' time, and there's a massive amount of work to get through beforehand."

"That sounds as if we shan't be seeing much of either of you," said the Mayoress resignedly. "Why is it one sees so little of the nicest people?" she sighed, assuming aloud that if Giles appeared, it was bound to be in Pip's company.

I wonder what she'll think when Giles and Stella announce that they're going to get married, thought Pip. Maybe it would be easier for her when they did, she reflected, at least it would save her this sort of misunderstanding, and by the time they were actually married she would be gone. Unconsciously her hand went up to touch the rose on her shoulder.

"It's feeling weary, too," Giles noticed her movement. "Never mind," he consoled, "there's plenty back at the nursery, you can make yourself a fresh buttonhole tomorrow."

"Flowers should never fade." The Mayoress evidently shared her feelings, that showed too clearly in her expressive face, a fact Pip was fully conscious of so that she summoned up a quick smile to mask her thoughts.

"I'll put it in water when I get back, it might revive." She could put it in the vase alongside the red rosebud, where it would fade beside its fellow, dying before it could open and reach its full beauty, as her own love must be allowed to die for want of its heart's desire to sustain it.

The haunting lilt of Weber's lovely music threaded through her thoughts, the notes entangling themselves among two coloured rosebuds, and ever afterwards the opening strains of "Invitation to the Waltz" would be inextricably linked for Pip with the perfume that came sweetly from her dainty spray. Giles opened his arms in invitation, his eyes smiling at her, willing her, despite her tiredness, to have this one last dance with him before, like Cinderella, the ball was ended, and her Prince Charming became once more her employer, and she the employed, linked only by the common bond of their mutual work and, she remembered wistfully, their shared love of roses.

They danced the last waltz in silence, lost in their own thoughts, the bright lights in the hall dimmed so that each found it difficult to see the other's face, leaving only the feeling of closeness between them that, however illusory, was still sweet, so that Pip dropped her head against Giles' shoulder, sensing his own bent over hers as she followed his steps more by instinct than anything else. Even the music from the orchestra was muted, giving precedence to the lone violinist who moved soft-footed among the dancers, his reed drawing piercing beauty from his throbbing strings in the dim half-light that seemed to Pip to be the start of the darkest night she would ever know.

CHAPTER EIGHT

Betsy had left a flask of hot coffee on her bedside table when Pip returned home, and for appearances' sake she took half a cupful. The scalding drink was sweet and strong, but it did nothing to relieve the weight that lay upon her spirits like a dark cloud.

I'll feel more cheerful after a night's sleep, she told herself robustly but with little inward conviction. It wasn't physical tiredness that ailed her, but perhaps a night's sleep might help to wipe away the sound of the cheerful invitations with which they had been showered as the dance ended, and the partygoers prepared to go home. The spate of "come along and see us," and "let's arrange a get-together soon", "how about it, Giles? You and Pip. . . ." to all of which Giles responded with a non-committal "Maybe soon, I'll get in touch." He didn't say "We'll get in touch". So that when she herself was similarly pressed by their well-meaning companions she hedged in her turn, unable to explain that if Giles did accept their invitations he would be accompanied by someone else.

Sleep, too, would take away, if only temporarily, the memory of the silent drive home, as silent as the last waltz, but without the feeling of closeness to one another, the exchange of ballroom for car dispelling the magic aura of the music, its spell broken by the practical necessity to concentrate on driving, so that Pip, disliking interruption herself when she was behind the wheel, forbore to speak. But Giles had no need to concentrate when he saw her to the door of Betsy's cottage, the entrance so close to that of his own home as to be but a step away. He had no need to be silent then, when he took her key from her fingers and fitted it into the lock; opened the door into the darkness beyond that seemed extra dark after the brilliance of the moon outside, despite the last embers of the sitting room fire showing faintly through the half open door into the hall. Most men would have taken advantage of such a moon, perhaps used it as a lighthearted excuse for a goodnight kiss, even if the girl was not the one they intended to marry. It would have been a fitting ending to the evening, as illusory as their closeness while they danced, and the assumption of Giles' friends that she was his chosen companion, but an ending nevertheless that would have rounded off a dream and made it complete.

Giles evidently preferred unfinished symphonies, she thought despondently. His carefree manner dropped from him like a cloak as they left the hotel, and the old shell of reserve closed about him once more, not so tightly, perhaps, that no chink showed through of the happy companion with whom she had spent the evening, but enough, nevertheless, to restrain his arm that remained loosely about her shoulders except for that one brief, impulsive moment when it tightened and started to turn her towards him, then as she lifted her face to his he checked himself and drew back, and the moment was lost, gone for ever like a bubble that bursts when it is touched by careless fingers, losing the iridescent beauty of its rainbow colours that return to the air which first gave them birth, leaving only an elusive memory of a beauty that might never have been.

Pip woke shivering, the tumbled bedclothes betraying an unquiet sleep that had brought oblivion, but gave her no real rest. "Brrr!" She gave the eiderdown a tug, which was all the shiny cover needed to slide it over the edge of the bed and on to the floor. "Oh, bother!" She reached for her dressing gown with frozen fingers, and remembered the flask of coffee that still stood nearly full on her bedside table. It should still be hot in the thermos. She poured some out and tasted it, and curled her hands round the cup gratefully, feeling the steaming drink course through her with a glow that gave her the courage to slide out of bed after the errant covers, propelled by a determination to remake her couch and gain whatever rest she could for the remainder of the night. She could not have been in bed for long, for the moon was still bright, its white light paled the heavy curtains, and she held up the alarm clock, seeking its luminous hands to tell her the time. The finger pointed to four o'clock, and she put it to her ear, but it was still ticking with an energy she found herself envying. Perhaps Giles had left the front lights on, she thought, though she had never noticed before that they shone on the windows with such a vivid effect. Carrying her cup of coffee, she walked across the room and pulled the curtains apart, puzzled by the hard, clear light that greeted her as she looked out. It lay across the nursery premises, outlining each small detail with a cold clarity, touching the tops of the greenhouses with tinsel brightness, and putting a halo round the edge of the clipped bushes that lined Betsy's path. It had not the ethereal effect of moonlight, that softens whatever it lies on with a magic touch, nor yet did it look like the yellow glow of lamplight. She craned her head round and saw that the front lights were in fact switched off, so they could not be responsible. This light had a hardness about it that was like – like – icing, she decided, like the bright sugar frosting of a birthday cake. Frosting. . . . She pressed her nose against the window pane, making a small, clear blob where it had misted over with the steam from her drink, and the sudden sharp moisture of her exhaling breath as realisation of what she was looking at gripped her with dismaying force.

"Frost!" It couldn't be, not at this time of the year. "Oh, my goodness, George's dahlias!" The entire nursery stock lay bedded out under the white rime, probably scorched black by now. He had probably put out the chrysanthemum cuttings too, she couldn't remember. That's the bulk of the cutting flowers for the autumn gone west, she thought, horrified at the effect the catastrophe would have on the selling section of the nursery, that relied on a plentiful supply of cut flowers to keep them viable. Each section had to be self-supporting, and without the cut blooms the selling section looked like having a poor year. It would happen when Giles was so worried about the proposed new road, she thought sympathetically. Why did trouble always have to find itself a companion? she wondered. He would have trouble enough soon if the plans for the road went ahead. The sheer effort, to say nothing of the expense of removing an entire nursery to new premises, apalled her. No doubt Giles would have coped well enough with that, she had discovered that difficulties were simply hurdles to be jumped in Giles' estimation, it was the potential loss of his home that was his Achilles heel. Still, there was nothing she could do about the dahlias now, or. . . . She took another look at the clock. Four o'clock, give or take a minute or two. It was after two when they had returned from the dance, and there was no sign of rime then. There was just a chance. . . .

She gulped down the last of her coffee and struggled into slacks and sweater over her pyjamas. A double layer would help to keep her warm, she thought, her hand seeking a nylon mac hung in her wardrobe, and a woolly cap with a bobble on the top that would keep her ears cosy. It was no use wearing gloves, her hands would have to put up with it, she decided callously. A pair of thick socks and gumboots completed her hurried dressing, and she ran downstairs as fast as she could without making a noise – there was no sense in disturbing the others as well. She was not even certain yet that her emergency measure would work, but she could not just stand by and not even bother to try.

Avoiding the gravel paths, she made for the neat grass edging that gave the front of the nursery such a trim appearance, and provided her now with silent running until she came to the potting shed, and the roll of hose-pipe that she sought. The door opened readily enough, and the hose reel turned silently on well oiled bearings the moment she pulled the end of the tubing. All Sam's tools were well oiled, she thought, blessing the elderly man's particular ways. Within minutes she had the other end coupled to the tap, and then she was running in the direction of the big, square nursery beds where George had put out the dahlias, and – yes – the chrysanthemum cuttings were out too, or some of them; there was a bed and a half of those.

Pip began to wish she had woken Sam to give her a hand, another hose fitted to the second tap would have been a help, but there was no time now. The small plants, so strong and green in yesterday's sunshine, look-ed pathetic even in the half light of the pre-dawn glow. At least it gets light early at this time of the year, she thought thankfully; she would soon be able to see better what she was doing. She raced back to the shed and turned the tap full on, and caught her foot against an empty bucket that she hadn't noticed was half rolled on its side against the door. It completed the rest of the journey to the concrete underneath with a clatter that was enough to wake the dead, she thought with exaspera-tion.

"Oh, stand up!" She sat it back on its base with a quick-tempered clank that she made no effort to silence. If the noise had penetrated the house walls the entire population of the nursery must be awake by now any-way. She took to her heels again to pick up the other end of the hose and play the jet on the wilting plants. Her thumb and forefinger were soon wet through and num-bed to the bone as she exerted pressure on the end to achieve a fine spray of sufficient force to wash the scorching rime from the leaves and stems. The air was bitterly cold, and she desisted long enough to pull the polo neck sweater up round her nose, so that it met the ribbing of her woolly cap, giving her a highwayman look as it left only the slits of her eyes showing between the two layers of knitting.

She tried not to think about the cold. It crept through her nylon mac and the thick woolly, penetrated her corduroy trousers, and made her feet and legs numb inside the knee-high rubber boots, but at least they kept her legs dry, for her hands were so cold that now and then the hose slipped between her fingers and gave her boots an unwelcome shower. She walked slowly, dragging the long cord of the hose with her, spraying, washing, her mind forcing her numbed body to activity, the necessity to clean the plants of their white covering a driving force that propelled her along the path beside the dahlia bed, on to the small chrysanthemum cuttings that if all had gone well would produce such glorious colours in the autumn, colours that she would not be here to enjoy – but she forced that thought away from her mind too. She must save Giles' plants. It was the least she could do for him; her only hope was that she was not too late.

"Why didn't you wake me?" Booted feet skidded to a halt beside her, and a voice harsh with concern sounded critically in her frozen ear.

"It looks as if I did," she retorted drily, through teeth that chattered. It was probably the clatter of the bucket that had roused her employer, but now he was here he needed no telling what to do. Within a time-scale that would not have disgraced the turnout of a crack fire brigade team, he had unrolled Sam's second hosepipe, coupled it to the other tap, and got it working in unison with her own.

"You take the chrysanth bed," she called, "I'll stay with the dahlias."

There were literally hundreds of plants, and every one

had to be thoroughly cleansed of their unwelcome covering if they were to survive, but somehow with Giles working beside her the task no longer seemed an impossible one, and even the morning did not seem quite so cold, although by the time the sun tipped the horizon Pip had lost all feeling in her legs and feet below her knees, and began to wonder if the pair of hands that she could see curled round the hosepipe did in fact belong to her.

"That's enough, we've done all we can." Giles took the hose from her hands. He had to uncurl her fingers from about it with his own, they were too cold for her to move them by herself. "We can't do anything more now," he told her quietly. "If there's any permanent damage done it'll make itself known in the next hour or two, when the sun gets up. We shall just have to wait and see," he added with stoic resignation.

Wait and see. That seemed to be the story of his life just now, Pip thought with quick sympathy. Wait and see if his plants would live. Wait and see if Stella could get a divorce. Wait for his rose to bloom before he could name it, and then see if it was successful at the County Show. And then wait and see what those nameless, faceless beings, "the planners", decided about the course of their new road, as to whether he would have a home and a nursery left to bother about any more.

"It seems such a waste." Somehow, the wilting plants at her feet seemed symbolic of all these things, and now the urgency was over, and they had done all that could be done, reaction set in, and her spirits joined the feet that she could not feel.

"Mother Nature isn't averse to a bit of vandalism now and then," her companion answered wryly, "but she usually has a purpose," he acknowledged. "The fact that out plants got in the way was just bad luck."

"I don't see. . . ." Pip's voice was indignant.

"I do." The man's tone was wearily philosophical, with

no bitterness evident at the waste of his stock. "We had a plague of fly last summer. Bugs of all sorts," he explained, with a countryman's bluntness. "We were spraying and dusting all the summer to try and keep them under some sort of control, and it was a losing battle," he added feelingly.

"So?" Pip felt too cold to bother about bugs of any sort.

"So, this frost will kill off most of this year's issue," he retorted, and to her amazement she detected a note of satisfaction in his voice. "The sunshine we've had over the last few days will have hatched out a lot of the over-wintering eggs, and the cold will destroy the new insects, so the pest population should be at least down to a more normal level this year, I hope. Just the same, I'm glad you spotted the frost," the satisfaction was unmistakable this time. "It would have been costly to replace all those plants."

"You might have to yet." Pip was determined to feel gloomy.

"I know, but at least they've got a chance now, and they wouldn't have had that if you'd gone back to bed and decided it was none of your business."

"Of course it's my business!" Pip was roused to a sharp retort. "I'm part of the team. It's my living as well," she reminded him forthrightly.

"I know." A hint of a smile curved his lips as he took the two hoses and began rolling them back on to their reels. "Is this what you fell over?" His smile widened as his foot kicked against the bucket on the floor of the shed.

"I was in too much of a hurry to bother where I was going," Pip confessed. "Do you think . . . ?" She didn't know how to ask, the words stuck in her throat. "What about your roses?" she blurted miserably. "You said the warmth had made them shoot early." What if the frost had destroyed his chances at the County Show? "All those years of work. . . ." She choked on her words, unable to go on.

"The frost might have destroyed the shoots, but it won't have harmed the bushes themselves," he told her quietly, his eyes closely scrutinising her face.

"But this year's bloom?" To survive the winter and get so near to June and have his hopes destroyed seemed doubly cruel to Pip.

"If they're badly damaged it'll mean waiting another year." Briefly his shoulders sagged, his disappointment showing through before he braced himself and turned to her briskly.

"Let's go and have a look," he suggested. "The walled garden doesn't usually get touched by frost, it's built on a rise for that purpose. Frost flows like water, it seeks the hollows and the low levels," he explained, telling her something she already knew, but she did not interrupt, but let him talk on, for he seemed to want to convince himself as well as her. "The monks built the walled garden so that they could benefit from early crops. They knew a thing or two, even if they did live hundreds of years ago," he paid his respects to the unknown gardeners whose work he now carried on, an unbroken chain of caring for the soil that fed them that made him at one with those silent, cowled figures who toiled in his plot so long ago. As he walked he talked, and Pip kept pace beside him. He had asked her to accompany him to the walled garden, that sanctuary to which he so rarely asked other people. He had only asked her because of an emergency, Pip realised, accepting the lack of privilege as it applied to her; nevertheless she wanted to go, wanted to see where Giles spent so many of his free hours, so that afterwards she could remember him there, in the spot that meant so much to him.

A round wrought iron ring opened the arch-shaped wooden doorway in the garden wall, the black metal shining with rime from the frost, its virgin halo instantly despoiled as Giles' fingers grasped it and turned it with a dull clank of metal against metal on the other side of the door, which itself opened silently, on smooth-running hinges. Sam's oil-can, guessed Pip with a quick inward smile; it was as much a part of her landlord as his concrete mixer, but the results were a daily blessing to everyone in the nursery, where a rusty squeak was a sound that was virtually unknown.

Her first quick impression as she stepped through the door into the walled enclosure inside was one of restfulness. The door shut behind them with a gentle thud, enclosing them in high walls of mellow brick, warm in colour like the walls of the house. It was easy to see why Giles spent so much of his time here; the industrious bustle of the nursery, and all the day-to-day problems that beset the head of a thriving business, seemed a world away from this peaceful spot. Short clipped emerald turf made the wide paths, in place of the harder wearing and more practical gravel outside the walls, softening the rather formal layout that was, Pip guessed, an inheritance from those former owners which Giles, loving the history of the place, was loath to disturb.

The wide green walkways led in sunray fashion into a central area of crazy paving on which a sundial rested as a silent reminder of passing hours to those who loitered there, uncaring of time. Fruit trees lined each wall, a row of cordon pears leaning at an angle like tipsy revellers, promising a juicy crop if their owner could deter the winged pirates who shared his liking for such good things. The south-facing wall held a fan-trained peach, that surely must be the origin of Betsy's delicious peach jam, and a quick glance at the other sides of the square confirmed Pip's guess that they carried plum and apple trees trained against the brickwork, both of which contributed to Betsy's generous store, along with the delicate flavouring from the herb garden, that lay immediately inside the gate. To Pip's knowledgeable eye the plot carried a specimen of every conceivable herb, some of which even she could not name, but which she guessed were descended from the original monastery garden that would have been the only source of medicine available in those days to a people who relied upon the gentle friars as the only source of knowledge or healing in a world that was dark with ignorance.

Beehives formed a white colony in a sheltered corner, and Pip envied the occupants their life in such a halcyon spot, though they were placed too close for comfort to a rustic seat, she thought warily.

"The frost hasn't reached here."

To Pip's surprise Giles did not go straight to his rose beds, which she could see at the far end of the garden, but branched off on a path that led to a magnificent magnolia tree in full bud against a corner of the wall, its creamy, infant blossom rising in ghostly tiers in the early light. Giles reached out and touched one of the buds with enquiring fingers.

"No, it isn't harmed," he reported with relief. "If the frost had come inside the walls, this tree would have been the first to show signs of it," he told Pip. "The walls have saved the garden. They've done so before."

"Aren't you going to check your rose bushes?" She spoke quietly; it would have been unseemly to raise one's voice here, she thought.

"Oh yes, we must make sure." He said "we", not "I", a concession that brought a faint warmth to her frozen frame as he rejoined her on the main path, and they turned together towards the far side of the garden. By common consent they both paused as they reached the sundial, seeking the faint shadow that was as yet scarcely discernible from the barely risen orb of light. Giles ran a slender finger across where the shadow lay, and Pip's eyes instinctively sought the source of the light, but as yet the high walls hid the rising sun. It would be some time before the shadowed garden lay in full light; the half light

141

of early dawn still lay over the quiet beds like a mysterious mantle whose presence turned them away in silence from their temporary stopping place.

"They're safe!"

Pip felt the tension in the man beside her as they approached the two borders closely bedded in rose bushes; heard his quick intake of breath given out in a sigh of relief that he could not quite control, and saw him visibly relax before he stooped and touched the nearest bush, gently, as he had touched the magnolia bud, seeking the answer that would set his fears at rest.

"They're safe," he repeated, and turned a face vivid with relief upwards to where Pip waited by his side, as anxious as he for the results of what had been years of work, that could so easily have been spoiled by one freak frost coming unexpectedly late after the weather had warmed to the advancing season, and everyone thought the winter had been left far behind. There was no sign of frost on any of the bushes, the tender young shoots that sprouted freely from the low pruned stems carried none of that sinister sparkle that was evident everywhere outside the walls, and Giles rose to his feet, tall and straight beside her, and new enthusiasm infused his voice that before had been taut with anxiety.

"Now for the County Show!" He smiled down at her, relief at this one deliverance driving away, if only for the moment, the even greater anxiety for the nursery's very existence which had hung precariously in the balance for too long, thought Pip, looking silently at the man's face that was fine-drawn, with evidence of too many sleepless nights in the faint hollows of his cheeks, and the lean frame that for its height should better fill out his clothes.

As he spoke the dawn silence of the garden was broken by a thrush, that landed on a high branch of the magnolia tree and immediately burst into song, the pure, clear notes piercingly sweet across the still air, a spontaneous hymn to the new morning that was like a breath of hope to the two people who paused to listen, strangely stirred by the wild music that has touched an inner chord in men's hearts throughout the ages, drawn by the joyous singer that has no thought of yesterday, but pours out its carol in a paean of gratitude for the gift of urgent, stirring life with another day, and hope for the days yet to come.

"It's an omen." There was a smile on Giles' lips, but his voice was serious, and Pip nodded, sobered in her turn, but feeling strangely calm, as she had not felt calm with Giles close to her for how long, now? It seemed an age, and this might only be a respite, but in this quiet garden even hearts must cease to ache, she thought, and wished she could stay here for ever, soaking in the peace that lay like a benediction across them while they remained within the sanctuary of its walls, making her feet reluctant to take her along the path that led back to the gate in the wall, and the world of reality that awaited them both on the other side. She paused beside a small evergreen bush, reaching out and snapping off a sprig, and burying her face in her hands to sniff the perfume that clung to her fingers from its aromatic oil.

"Rosemary."

"That's for remembrance," quoted Giles softly, and Pip flinched, her heart rawly awake to the fact that for her all this soon would be nothing but a memory, something to cherish and look back upon, but the reality of it belonging to someone else.

"My grandmother used rosemary to flavour her home-made lard." She had to come back to reality quickly, her feeling of peace shattered, and desperately aware of his closeness to her, so that she must grasp at mundane things to steady her before she betrayed her feelings in a way that could only bring embarrassment to her companion, and mortification to herself.

"Now you've spoiled it," Giles chided her, but there was a laugh in his voice to which she could respond with a flippancy that covered her thoughts, so that he might not guess what they were and add humiliation to her unhappiness. "Now back to the frost." He opened the gate and put his hand on her shoulder, a light, impersonal touch, meant to steer her through in front of him, and nothing else, although he did not immediately loose his grasp of her as he bent to make sure the catch homed into place so that the cold air did not reach the warmer area inside the walls.

"Heavens! What a difference," Pip gasped as the frozen scene greeted them, it was like walking into another world. True, the air inside the walled garden had been cold, but in their brief sojourn there so much seemed to have happened that they might have been there for weeks instead of minutes, so that the return to the icy world of the general nursery plots hit her with an almost physical shock, like that of a sleeper waking to find himself on a different planet.

"It's hard to believe, isn't it? But it's happened before like this, though we've never been rescued in quite such a gallant fashion," he teased her, and this time the hand that grasped her shoulder tightened, as if its owner would hug her to him, but thought better of it, and let his hand stay loosely there, linking them by shared work, and nothing more. "The sun's up." He turned her to face the east, where a pageant of colour enough to bewilder even the most skilled artist flaunted streamers of brilliant light across the cold background, tinting the whitened world underneath with a gentle rose pink in a brief illusion of warmth that would as quickly fade, leaving behind a sense of loss as the sun continued on its journey that took it away from the bed of colour in which it now rested. Their lives would separate in just such a way, thought Pip wistfully, hers and Giles, though it would be she who would have to travel, leaving Giles behind her in the colourful surroundings of the nursery, a southern landscape that her northern heart had come to think of as home. That, too, was an illusion, and a dangerous one she acknowledged, but it was too late now to pretend it was anything less, and the roots that she would have fain put down into this stranger soil were to be torn up before they had had time to take hold, a process that she knew would cause a cruel wound that would probably take many years to heal.

"Eh, Gaffer, why didn't you wake me!"

Sam puffed round the corner of the wall, his booted feet with the laces still undone clattering on the gravel in his haste, and dismay writ large on his normally cheery face. "All them dahlias!" he groaned.

"I didn't wake myself until Pip fell over your galvanised bucket," Giles retorted, "and I think the dahlias are safe," he relented. "Pip woke up and saw the frost, and didn't wait to be told what to do. We should have lost the lot if it hadn't been for her," he gave credit handsomely. "I only came on the scene after all the activity was over, or nearly so," he comforted Sam, who still looked upset. "There was no time to waste knocking people up," he begged the elderly man's understanding. "Pip was in charge, she was busy coping with the dahlias, and she sent me to deal with the chrysanth cuttings," he explained.

"It wouldn't have been any use waking you, Sam," Pip butted in gently. "There are only two hosepipes, and they were both in use." Giles had made it sound as if she was being bossy, she thought with quick resentment, her earlier peace destroyed, and the harsh realities of the working day lapping about her once more, bidding for attention with a clamour that would soon drown even the song of the thrush, she thought mournfully, with a reluctance to return to the bustle of her daily round that was alien to her normal enthusiasm.

"Come and look for yourself," Giles coaxed Sam, "you'll see then that there was nothing more any of us could do. If there's damage done, it's irreparable, and we'll just have to cope with the consequences as best we can." He turned towards the dahlia beds, and Pip intervened quickly.

"Do up your bootlaces, or you'll stumble," she told her landlord, for frost or no frost, it would not help anyone if Sam fell and injured himself, and Giles would be short-handed by one after the County Show. He did not know that yet, and she could not tell him, but womanlike she looked ahead and guarded against difficulties before they could arise. If lack of staff hit the nursery before she left, she realised that she would not be able to justify her own departure, which might solve a problem for Giles but would make an even bigger one for herself.

"If you say they're all right, then I don't need to look. They're all right," Sam stated positively, mollified by Giles' consideration for his feelings, and obediently bending down to pull the laces of his boots tight. "Me fingers am that cold, I can't rightly tie 'em," he grumbled, knotting nevertheless in his usual tidy fashion.

"We're all frozen," admitted Pip with a shiver, conscious of her own discomfort now the action was over.

"Then come in and have your breakfast," the elderly man bade her. "An' the wife says you'd better come too, Gaffer, the fire's hotter in our kitchen than it is in the house." He always called Giles' part of the dwelling "the house". "You'd do better to have a good roast while you eat, or you'll both catch your death," he bullied them, with more than a hint of Betsy in his manner, but they forbore to smile, suddenly glad of the coddling, and the roaring flames that greeted them as they stepped through the kitchen door.

"Strip off your wet things," Betsy bade them as soon as they were inside. "And your jackets," she insisted. "It'll let the warmth soak through." She was right as usual. Pip held out her hands to the hot glow that emanated from the kitchen grate, and shamelessly put her socked feet into the hearth, screwing her face up as the blood began to run freely, and painfully, back into her toes.

"Ooh, I've got the hot-aches!" she complained, but she kept them there for the blessed comfort of the warm bricks, and Betsy brought her a bowl of porridge to put on her knee.

"Stay where you are and eat it," she forestalled her attempt to rise and come to the table. "You too, Mr. Giles," she told him, in a tone that discouraged disobedience, and Pip grinned across the hearth as her employer meekly sat down on the stool opposite to her and followed her example.

"I daren't do otherwise," he grinned back, good-humouredly accepting her silent jibe, and contentedly began on his breakfast.

"Am I late?" Stella poked a puzzled face round the door. "Are we having breaking in here?" Her tone was disapproving, and for a brief instant Pip saw a frown flash across Giles' forehead.

"Just for this morning," he retorted firmly before Betsy could speak. It would not have occurred to Stella to save her landlady a few steps, no matter what crisis hit the household. She made her reluctance to join them in the kitchen obvious as she lingered in the doorway until Pip began to feel uncomfortable, and Giles' frown returned.

Stella's already practising being lady of the manor, Pip criticised her colleague silently, but it was not her business to intervene. She stole a glance at Sam's face, and almost laughed out loud. The sound of her landlord's familiar growl was absent, but the growl had settled on his face in an expression so unmistakable that Pip could almost hear it. Betsy's lips had vanished in a thin line, and the atmosphere became tense.

"Oops, sorry! It was Punch, he pushed me."

Skippy saved the day as she clattered downstairs in the nick of time and headed hungrily in the direction of the kitchen, with the eager mongrel as usual close behind her.

147

"I thought you were going in too," she apologised, disentangling herself from the dark-haired girl whom she had propelled willy-nilly into the room from behind, so that they both ended up side by side against the table.

"Sit down, now," Betsy hastily slid two place settings on to the cloth and defused the situation with a quick grasp at opportunity. "Come and eat your porridge while it's hot," she coaxed. Few could resist her motherly persuasion, and although Stella still looked put out she sat down, and Betsy signalled to her husband to join them with a no-nonsense jerk of her head that brought him meekly to his place at her side. "Into the corner, Punch." She disposed of the dog to his blanket by the hearth, where he obediently curled up until it was his turn to be fed.

"Did you like the dance?" Skippy screwed round on her stool so that she could talk to Pip and eat her porridge at the same time, a feat which she managed miraculously without a spill. "Were the dresses pretty? You said you'd let me have the painting today." She chattered on, unconscious of any strain between the grown-ups, her barrage of eager questions directed impartially at Pip and Giles whom she regarded in a puzzled fashion as they remained beside the fire. "Are you poorly?" In her young eyes people were only excused eating at the table if they were practically at death's door.

"No, we're fine," Giles smiled across at her, "but we've been up for quite a while washing frost off the plants, and we're just trying to thaw out. I'll bet you haven't even looked outside yet," he teased her. "It's all white."

"Has it snowed?" Incredulous hope shone on Skippy's freckled face.

"No, thank goodness!" retorted Giles fervently. "The frost's quite bad enough as it is. But we're cold from using the hoses," he explained seriously. He never talked down to the child, Pip noticed, treating her quick intelligence with the respect it deserved.

"We had to get up and go out in an awful hurry," Pip added a spice of drama for her.

"I wondered why you'd still got your 'jamas on," the six-year-old remarked complacently, and Pip realised with a blush of dismay that a good two inches of pink nylon and dainty lace showed between the top of her socks and her trouser bottoms that she had automatically hitched up as she sank on to the low fireside seat. The grin on Giles' face clattered her porridge bowl on to the hearth as she hastily set it down and pulled her socks up over the offending nightwear.

"I'll change as soon as I'm warm," she promised, "and you can come with me and collect your picture at the same time," she skilfully sidetracked another remark from Skippy that she decided she didn't want the whole room to hear, and hoped her companions would take the warmth she felt on her cheeks as coming from the heat of the fire. Her hope was short-lived when she looked up and met the mischievous glint in Giles' eyes, and she looked away hastily, burying her nose in her coffee cup as a quick refuge from her confusion.

"That's the paper boy. Gran, can I go?" Skippy was already off her stool at the sound of the familiar newsboy whistle that came from outside the door. She waited with her eye on her grandmother for the expected permission, and Betsy nodded indulgently.

"Run along, if you want to."

It was the same routine every morning, Pip had heard it through the open door into the dining room a dozen times. Skippy made it her business to collect her grandfather's newspaper from the front door of the cottage morning and evening, a pleasant ritual in which Punch always joined. Pip noticed with a quick smile that the mongrel, too, looked up at Betsy for permission before leaving his blanket in the corner and padding after the child.

"Drop it, Punch! Let go!" Skippy's voice rose with shrill pleading from somewhere near the front door. "Ooh, look, you've torn the corner." She reappeared smoothing the morning issue of the local newspaper to mitigate the damage inflicted by her wagging companion, and her glance caught the photograph emblazoned on the front page. She stopped dead in her tracks, her eyes widening.

"It's Pip . . . 'n Mr. Giles. Look, Gran! Isn't she pretty?" The youngster homed to her grandmother's side and spread the newspaper on the table, a breach of behaviour that under normal circumstances would have earned a swift rebuke, but as Betsy's eyes fell on the picture the correction faded on her lips, and her homely face beamed with pleasure.

"My, but that's nice," she enthused. "Look at that, now, Sam," she bade her husband, and held the newspaper high for him and the others to see.

It was the picture the young reporter had taken, the one Pip thought would come out with her eyes closed since the flash of his bulb had taken her unawares. She glanced at it quickly to confirm her fears, and realised with a sigh of relief that they were groundless, but her complacency was short-lived. The reporter had caught her just as Giles had said "Smile!" and she had looked up into his face as he spoke, so that the camera caught them gazing into one another's eyes in an attitude that was totally misleading, thought Pip, a cold feeling gripping her as she thought of the reaction of Giles' friends upon seeing such a picture, attractive as it undoubtedly was. The photographer had chosen his background well, setting his subjects against a flower-decked archway through which they had just strolled, with the pale glow of a just visible chandelier from the room beyond outlining them. Pip was stood slightly in front of Giles, her fair head in sharp contrast against the stark black and white of his evening clothes, her dress swirling out about her slender figure from her movement as she turned to her escort. It was a delicate, appealing picture, catching the fairytale mood of the evening. It was. . . .

"Romantic!" drawled Stella cynically. And her black eyes laughed.

CHAPTER NINE

THE floral figures that had occupied so much of Pip's time and thought were faded, the frames stripped of their erstwhile beauty and relegated to the storeroom. Her two roses, which Giles had given so casually, were faded too, but they had not been discarded as the cladding of the frames had been discarded. The two buds, the yellow and the red, were carefully pressed between tissue leaves in a treasured volume of poetry that Pip kept in her room, and that would in future provide its reader with a wistful memory when she turned to the familiar lines.

The picture in the newspaper was not so easily laid aside, though she had rescued a copy of that, too, and it resided with her roses, so that she could one day draw it out when time had eased the hurt and live again the golden moments when she danced in Giles' arms. There had been several pictures of herself and Giles in the various local newspapers, but none so appealing as the one taken by the young reporter. The accent of the other pictures was mainly on the Lord Mayor and his lady, and although Pip and Giles appeared in several of them they were not the central figures. Much had been made in the newspapers of the floral display at the hotel, which brought the nursery a lot of valuable publicity, and several weeks later enquiries were still coming in from organisers of large functions in areas far removed from their own county. Giles was elated at the success of their efforts, and Pip felt justifiably pleased, though she could not respond to his optimistic look at the future.

"There's the County Show, and who knows what's to

follow?" he enthused.

There would be nothing to follow, at least not for her, though Pip felt that this was hardly the moment to tell him so. He had enough on his mind with the threat of the new road without her spoiling his small triumph now.

The reaction of the nursery staff was predictably joyful. Coppers were expended on newspapers by people who normally never read one, so that the village shop ran out and had to get in another supply. Copies of the photographs appeared on the walls of the worksheds, the one of Pip and Giles together being far more numerous than the others, and Pip saw to her embarrassment that one of the women had framed her copy with a strip of the ribbon they used in making up wedding bouquets.

What on earth will Giles think? she wondered, wishing she had not taken her usual short cut through the worksheds that morning, but there was no escape now, and she faced the badinage bravely enough, knowing it to be friendly.

"Wish I was young and slim again, don't you, 'Ilda?" The buxom owner of the newspaper cutting looked at its subject enviously.

"And in love," her companion retorted with a grin.

"Well, aren't you?" Giles appeared on the scene, taking the same short cut as Pip, and eyed his two employees quizzically. "You're both married," he reminded them. "I thought love was supposed to give a lifetime's wear?" His eyes crinkled with laughter, but there was an underlying seriousness in his tone that caught Pip's ear. His love would wear for a lifetime, she had no doubt. But Stella's love? What did he think of her capacity to love for a lifetime? she wondered. How did he relate his own principles to her divorce? He would have had to reach a compromise somewhere, she realised, but it must have been a painful one.

"I can get through now, thanks, George." She slipped past the wagon of seed boxes which the foreman was moving across the aisle, and that had successfully prevented her from reaching the door on the other side. Without looking round she fled outside, not caring whether Giles was following or not so long as she escaped his eyes that seemed to bore into her very thoughts, and those he must not be allowed to read.

The photographs were still tacked on to the workshed walls, but the nine days' wonder of the publicity had subsided, and the talk in the nursery now was all of the County Show. The success of the function at the Manor Hotel acted as a spur, and the nursery staff bombarded Pip with offers of help which, if she had accepted them all, would have emptied the premises of people during the period of the Show. To keep their interest alive, and their minds off the fact that by the end of the year there might not be a nursery to work at, Giles let it be known that he would name his rose on the day of the Show, and a spate of suggestions followed which eventually provided another article for the young reporter, who found it profitable to patronise the village public house that was also a rendezvous for the employees of Shieldons. Giles cast an indulgent eye on the column presented one morning by a worried George.

"Didn't think it was generally known about your rose, Gaffer. Seems as if it's leaked, like."

"It's my own fault, George," Giles reassured him, glancing down the report. "I deliberately let it be known about the rose, and it seems to have boosted morale no end," he said with satisfaction. "You must admit it was at a pretty low ebb here when the papers first printed the report about the new road. They might as well do us a good turn and print something helpful for a change."

"Better than that sloppy write-up about the elm tree," grunted the foreman. He still had not forgiven the *Echo* for what he regarded as unwarranted interference on that score.

"That's over and done with. Anyway, the elm decided

its fate for itself," Giles replied, falling into step beside his foreman. "By the way," he annexed Pip and Stella as they crossed paths on their way to the cottage. "can you manage on your own for a few days, Pip? Stella and I have got to go to London," he enlarged, as Pip bent an enquiring eye on George, whom she had never known to leave the nursery except to go home to his meal at night. "It'll leave you on your own," he said apologetically.

"Pip won't mind, will you?" Stella's tone intimated that she didn't really care whether Pip minded or not.

"Of course I can manage." Pip spoke quickly, deliberately scornful to crush the sudden lurch her heart gave at the news. "The rush won't start on the Show work for another week yet." She would have to get used to the thought of Giles being with Stella. It would be easier when she was gone from the nursery and did not have to meet them every day, and see them together, but there was still the time to be lived through until she could leave. "I'll manage fine," she repeated robustly, with a force that made the man's eyes rest thoughtfully on her uptilted chin. She would have to learn to manage without Giles permanently soon, so she might as well get used to it now, she told herself bleakly. She could a lot easier get used to doing without Stella, although since the dark-haired girl had spent part of Easter away with Giles she had become a lot more likeable, Pip admitted honestly, but she saw as little of her outside working hours as before, Stella going off into town a good deal, and spending the better part of the evenings when she did remain at home in using the telephone. Pip assumed she was making arrangements for her wedding – or for her divorce? It was difficult to decide, and characteristically Stella declined to comment. Skippy was a help; she demanded even more of Pip's attention than before, which she was willingly given, and her eager outpourings about the arrangements for her mother's coming wedding to George, at which she was to be a bridesmaid, side-tracked Pip's attention. Skippy's mother confided in her too, asking her advice on a dozen different matters, and between the two of them Pip grasped gratefully at the distraction that left her with little time to think about her own problems.

"Will you look after my rose bushes for me while I'm away?"

Pip thought at first Giles had spoken to George. It was only after he repeated his request that she realised he had asked her to look after his roses. Her surprise must have been evident in her face, because his eyebrows described an enquiring arc.

"If you'd rather not . . . ?"

"Of course I'll look after them." How could he think she would rather not? "It's only – well, they are special. . . ." What if something went wrong and spoiled his chances at the Show? Her mind boggled at the thought, and she almost wished he hadn't asked her, but she knew that was not true. She was glad he had asked her, glad he trusted her that far, so that she would at least leave the nursery feeling that she had had some share in the success of his rose. And if anything did go wrong, she thought, with bitter amusement, it would solve one problem for her. She would not need to give in her notice, for Giles would undoubtedly sack her on the spot.

"Don't look so worried." Giles' voice was teasing. "Rose bushes scratch, they don't bite! All I shall want you to do," he instructed, "is to give them one feed while I'm away, and while you're about it keep a lookout for fly. I don't want holes punched in the petals by a lot of hungry greenfly. And I'll leave the feed, and a mixture of spray, ready made up for you," he forestalled her question. "That way you won't be afraid of using the wrong mixture," he coaxed.

"In that case you've got a volunteer," she said promptly, with such patent relief that it drew a spontaneous laugh from the two men, though the amusement died from Giles' eyes as they returned to Pip's face.

"I'd regard it as a favour," he told her quietly, as if still conscious of her earlier hesitation.

"It seems a lot of fuss to make over a few roses," Stella remarked casually. "It isn't as if they're anything special, like orchids. They're not all that expensive."

That was the criterion she applied to most things, Pip realised. She didn't seem to understand that a price could be exacted in any other coin beside that of money.

"When are you going?" Pip steered the conversation away from the roses on to safer ground, not daring to look at Giles' face. Didn't Stella realise how she must hurt? she wondered angrily. Was she so self-centred that she could not know how much Giles' dream meant to him? Or knowing, could not care?

"I'm starting about mid-morning." Giles' voice was even; maybe he had trained himself not to let it show that he cared. "It's no good starting before," the amusement was back, "my passenger doesn't come awake until then, and I'll want her to navigate part of the way for me."

Perhaps Stella was taking him to see her people. That would explain Giles being uncertain of the way, probably among a lot of local by-roads. He was sufficiently seasoned in travelling to tackle any other sort of journey without assistance. Well, she would go out herself while they were both away, Pip vowed. It would while away the evenings when she didn't want to be alone with her thoughts, after Skippy's chatter had been silenced by bedtime, and she was left with a couple of hours or so to fill in before she sought her own room. She would ring and book a seat at the theatre at Mossly. There was a new play on, and it was ages since she had seen one, it would make a pleasant change. If she booked her seat, she would have to go, she blackmailed herself.

Her good intentions were foiled after dinner by Stella, who annexed the telephone in the hall. There was no instrument in her flat, and she seemed in no hurry to remove herself from the chair which she had dragged with her, and proceeded to make herself comfortable and dial number after number in solid succession. Giles had always insisted that they make whatever calls they wished free of charge, a facility for which Pip was grateful, and used sparingly, conscious that someone else was paying for the calls, but which Stella characteristically used ad lib with no thought of limiting the time of her conversations, which tended to be protracted to an extent that sparked growls of disapproval from Sam. These, too, went unheeded, and tonight she left the door of the sitting-room open, which gave Pip the added embarrassment of overhearing part of the conversation whether she wanted to or not. She got up once to shut the door, but it looked like pointed rudeness, so she returned to her chair, for the same reason unwilling to turn up the volume of the television, and so drown the words from outside the door.

"Yes, I know, but we can't make any arrangements yet . . . not until after he comes back." Stella's lazy drawl went on and on, punctuated by gaps in which the conversationalist at the other end took his or her turn. So by the time Giles returned, and presumably Stella with him, she would have some idea when her divorce would be finalised, and they would be free to marry, thought Pip, unable to avoid gleaning knowledge which she would rather have been without. Somehow, knowing made it so final. "Oh yes, by that time he'll have got what he wants, I hope." Her tone was patronising. That would be Giles' rose, thought Pip, hoping that he would, in fact, get what he wanted and win the first prize. It seemed unnatural of Stella not to be even the least bit interested, since she must have known the rose would be named after her. To nine women out of ten such a naming would be a signal honour, appreciated for the affection that bestowed it, if not for the rose itself. "Oh, I shall be glad when all this messing about is over, and we can settle down. . . ."

Pip waited to hear no more. She gathered up her magazine that she realised now she had been trying to read upside down – the printed words were a daze before her eyes, and either way up made no difference, she thought impatiently – and fled for the stairs, gaining the sanctuary of her room and slamming the door behind her before the tears started to flow, and her heart poured out its misery on the pillow that over the last few weeks had become used to receiving such outbursts, although it had no comfort to offer beyond its own plump softness.

She deliberately went out early the next morning, taking the van for a round of calls that she had no need to do until after lunch, so that she should not see Giles and Stella depart together.

"It's a pity you went off so soon, Miss Pip." Betsy gave her her lunch and the news at the same time. "Mister Giles came looking for you. He said to tell you he'd left the feed for the roses, and the spray you wanted, in the corner of your workroom. He's marked them so's you'll know which is which." Betsy was well versed in the importance of such things in the life of the nursery. "He started off not long after you went," she chatted on, cheerfully unconscious that Pip shrank even from the mention of his name. She had steeled herself not to think of him while he was away, and here was Betsy. . . . Suddenly she did not want her lunch, but under her landlady's gimlet eye she made a pretence of eating. "Mr. Giles said he didn't want to go, but he said it was – it was – important to our future," Betsy remembered triumphantly.

Not their future – Giles' and Stella's future. And if Giles hadn't wanted to go, he was probably worried about his rose trees, which meant he did not really trust

159

her to look after them after all, thought Pip miserably. She gave up and laid aside her knife and fork, and making a quick excuse she refused Betsy's offer of sweet and coffee and made her way outside, out of range of her landlady's shrewd eyes. Instinctively her feet turned towards the path that led to the walled garden, her troubled mind seeking the solace which she had found there before. She could hear Skippy's bright chatter approaching round a corner of the greenhouses; from the sound of the voice that answered her she was with Sam. Pip felt guilty at not waiting for the child, who she knew would have enjoyed going to the walled garden with her, but just now she urgently wanted to be on her own, to give herself time to compose her feelings, and assert the stern self-discipline which was an essential part of her character, so that she could at least put on a show of cheerfulness in front of the others, and avoid the comment and possible questions that she had seen lurking in Betsy's eyes when she left the table. In Giles' garden, when she walked there with him, time had seemed to stand still, and she put her hand to the iron ring on the door, resisting an impulse to go on tiptoe, as if she might catch some secret of the garden unawares.

When she stepped inside she saw to her delight that the garden itself had not stood still. On the morning of the frost, the sheltered plot had stood on the brink of early summer, poised in bud like the magnolia tree, its full beauty as yet not revealed. Now, the tide of blossom was in full flood. The magnolia tree was already past its best, but enough showed of its former glory to make it still a noble sight, and the walls seemed to be padded in a thick cushion of fruit blossom that made the staid brickwork look as if it had donned a party dress. A faint hum permeated the air around her, and Pip realised that it came from the inmates of the hives in the far corner of the garden, busily engaged among the blossom, and in a cotoneaster bush beside the door. Pip would have thought the tiny pink flowers of the cotoneaster to be too small to attract the energetic workers, but despite its insignificant blossoms the whole bush was astir with life. A thrush, equally busy, and probably the one that had sung so sweetly to the frosty air, hunted along the lawn edge, and having filled its beak took off and homed to a laurel bush, where it evidently had a nest of young ones.

All the garden, trees, plants and creature life, seemed to be engaged on working for their own particular harvest, be it fruit or fledgling, and Pip felt suddenly left out of the busy order of things of which she was normally so much a part. She made her way to the seat in the corner, not pausing at the sundial, and uncaring that the seat was close to the beehives; the inmates were too busy, she guessed, to pay any attention to a human intruder. She sank down on to the wooden slats, fingering the warm roughness of the wood underneath her, willing the peace that she had felt in the garden before to come to her now, but either her mood was not receptive or she had come at a time when the garden was too busy about its own affairs to heed the needs of a mere human, the peace she had felt so strongly then was denied to her now, and she rose from the seat restless and unsatisfied. Perhaps it was because she walked the paths alone, without Giles, her very longing denying her the solace that the garden might otherwise offer. She sought the rose beds, trying to distract her mind with practicalities, a ploy that was successful when she saw the tight buds that rose from strong shoots on every bush. The bushes themselves were in perfect condition. Pip knelt and investigated the nearest ones, but they all seemed clean, with no sign of infestation visible on any of the ones nearest to her. Just the same, she decided, she would spray them as Giles had asked her to.

"I'll do them tomorrow," she told George when she met him as he came through the gate.

"You're good at washing down," the foreman retorted. "Those dahlia plants are doing fine and the chrysanth cuttings. If it hadn't been for you we'd have lost the lot."

"Well, we won't lose the roses." Pip was adamant. "The bushes look healthy enough, and they're smothered in buds," she told him enthusiastically.

"The results of the County Show mean a lot to Mr. Giles," George said seriously. "It could be a deciding factor where he goes if his holding here is taken over for the new road. Whether to generalise as he does here," he enlarged to Pip's enquiring look, "or to specialise in roses only. I don't think that's a good idea myself, puts all your eggs in one basket, like," he commented thoughtfully.

"He could expand the rose business here, he's got plenty of land," retorted Pip. "He could go in for less of the ordinary stuff, and more specialist work, that way he could keep the business viable and follow his hobby at the same time."

"That's what he'll do, I reckon. That is, if he can stay on here."

"We won't even think of him moving," Pip rejoined firmly. She must try to cheer George up; she was feeling too low herself to shoulder his fears as well. "You've been to the Show before, I came too late for it last year. What sort of area are we likely to be allocated for our display?"

"A good sized one. I heard from the organisers only this morning." George reached into his pocket and pulled out a bundle of papers that looked decidedly the worse for wear from their temporary residence. "Ah, here it is." He leafed through them and produced an official-looking form, and held it out for Pip to see. "It'll be under canvas, of course, but we've got all the one plot to ourselves, so it'll give us plenty of scope. I'm going up there tomorrow," he told her. "If you'd like to come along and have a look at the ground it'll give you some idea of the background we're working against, and the map on the back of the form here will tell us just where we're to be placed."

"Thanks, I'd like to." It would be something to look forward to, and company as well, she decided, removing herself to bed that night after a lonely and unsuccessful visit to the theatre at Mossly. The play was an indifferent one, the hero and heroine poorly cast, and supported by a cast who would have been better advised to seek other employment, thought Pip waspishly, seeking her transport almost before the last curtain had fallen, and rejecting the idea of remaining in town for supper. Going to the theatre on her own had been lonely enough, without prolonging the misery of the evening when she didn't have to. The thought of Giles and Stella together had intruded between herself and the actors, so that she could scarcely remember even now what the company had been trying to portray, and she greeted George's presence the next morning with wholesome relief. His homely face and down-to-earth outlook were what she needed just now.

"Can I come too?" Skippy laid her claim to her future stepfather, happily certain of his response.

"If Miss Pip doesn't mind?" Receiving Pip's smiled assent, he hoisted the child up into the van in the middle of the seat. "Mind and sit still, now. Back into the house, Punch," he refused the mongrel. "I can't take you both with me."

"Will there be sideshows?" Skippy wriggled happily up to Pip on the bench seat.

"There'll be nothing there yet, unless another show's being held?" she questioned George.

"No, the ground's bare. The County Show isn't for another two weeks and a bit – three Saturdays and Sundays." George placed it for their small companion in terms of time off from school, which was the only way Skippy counted.

"There'll be lots of things to see when it does come,"

Pip consoled her. "Prize animals for the competitions, and maybe some show jumping to watch as well. Do they extend to that here, George?" The shows over the border were usually a conglomeration of all the arts and crafts, sports and pastimes as well as the more serious side of agriculture, but this one might be different.

"It'll all be there," George assured his two passengers, swinging the van on to the road away from the village. "Helicopter flights too, from what I've heard. If you're not too frightened to go up, I might even take you," he teased.

"I'll go!" The response from the child was immediate.

"I won't!" Pip's response was equally quick, and just as decided. "I like my feet on the ground." She made no excuse for cowardice, and her companions laughed.

"It'll only be a flip round the ground, I expect. A chance to look at the whole Show at once without making your feet ache," George grinned.

"I'll settle for a pair of comfortable shoes," laughed Pip, eyeing the bare green acres into which George turned the van, space that would soon take on the carnival activity of the Show.

"Have you finally decided on what display you're going to put on?" George pulled the bundle of forms from his pocket that looked even worse for wear than they had the day before, and prepared to descend opposite a block of buildings, the main door of which carried the brief notice "Show Office".

"Yes, we've settled for an old-fashioned garden," Pip replied. "Giles used a bit of psychology there," she admitted honestly. "When I suggested it, he said it would be a good idea to give people a peaceful spot to sit in for a while, and rest their feet away from the hurly-burly of the Show ground. While they're enjoying a sit-down, they'll have time to really look at the display round them, instead of just glancing at it as they normally do," she chuckled.

Unconsciously she had based her idea for the Show on the walled garden at the nursery, using in a modified form the same sunray plan for her layout. This time there was no need for her to paint a picture to guide her, as she had for the function at the Manor Hotel. The Show "garden" would be made up of container-grown shrubs taken when in the full beauty of their bloom, and graph paper and a lot of careful thinking were all that were required to make the desired layout. That, and the imagination to visualise the colourful results.

"We'd thought of having an archway at the entrance, so that people would have to come through to see what lay beyond." She had used the same sense of mystery that she herself felt when she first approached the door in the garden wall, not knowing what lay beyond it, and longing to see, an urge that she hoped would tempt visitors to the Show to walk through the arch and take the paths that would be laid out inside the tent, leading to a central bower that would come upon the walker unawares. The paths themselves would be deeply bordered by a multi-mixture of shrubs of all kinds, and would open out through another arch into a small circle that would contain nothing but roses. A similar seat to the one in the walled garden would be placed among them, though Pip resisted a mischievous temptation to include a beehive. Her own cautious approach to the striped honey-gatherers might well be shared by others, and a bee-sting was not the way Giles would want their efforts remembered by, they hoped, an interested public.

"We've chosen all the perfumed roses for the display." Memory could be stirred as well by perfume as by sight, and George nodded his approval.

"I don't reckon a rose is a rose unless it's got a smell," he shared her feelings.

"We'll need that small fountain from the store, too," she warned him. "Giles said there's an adequate supply of power laid on here from which we can run it."

"There usually is, but I'll check just in case." The foreman slid out of the van and made for the office.

She could substitute a sundial if necessary, but she would rather have a fountain, the play of water would give a sense of life and movement to the static display, and would also serve to cool the air, which would benefit the flowers under the stuffy canvas.

"That's settled." George returned and hauled himself back into the driving seat. "You can have your fountain," he told her. "The Show secretary said they'd provide us with a couple of power units – big batteries, like," he enlightened her feminine ignorance of such technicalities. "We can run off one and use the other as a spare if necessary. Where are you going to put Mr. Giles' roses?" he asked. "The special ones, I mean?"

"I'd thought of putting a container full in the centre of the bower at the back, right opposite where the paths come together under the arch, so that whoever walks in will look straight at them. I'll use one of those mock stone pedestals from the store, and fix the container on top."

"Sounds as if you're going to have an unveiling ceremony," the foreman teased.

"Well, aren't we?" she retorted. "It'll be a similar thing, announcing the name of the rose." She could visualise the container now, holding not too many but just enough of the most perfect buds, unnamed and awaiting what she knew Giles hoped would be a double bestowal, of the coveted prize, and the name of the rose at the same time.

The warmth was making one or two of the buds show colour already, she noticed when she sprayed them later, paying careful attention to the thick green mossing of the stem, that however attractive to the human eye made as good a cover as thick grassland to the minute greenfly that could yet ruin Giles' hopes of a prize.

"When you think of the number of hazards a gardener faces, you wonder why anyone bothers," she marvelled to George, who followed her into the garden and cast an interested eye on the progress of the bushes. Nevertheless she returned to give them their feed the next day, and resisted an almost overpowering impulse to pick one of the buds as a keepsake. This might be the last time she ever came to the walled garden. Resolutely she turned her back on the buds and picked up the sprayer. She would have to make the sprig of rosemary do; it was pressed along with the two rosebuds Giles had given her, and the photograph from the newspaper. It wasn't fair to pick one of the special buds, although there were many to choose from, but Giles would undoubtedly notice if she clipped one off. He was due back the next day and the whitened stem end would show.

With a rush of longing she wished that Giles was back at the nursery, back in charge of his own plants – suddenly the responsibility of the garden seemed a heavy burden on her shoulders – or just back, so that she could see him walking the paths, hear his voice as he talked to George or Sam, or occasionally to her when he wanted to make some point clear, or just casually pass the time. She saw too little of Stella to miss her presence, but how she missed Giles! Every moment of the day she was conscious of an emptiness that was even worse than the emptiness inside her when he was there, and scarcely noticed her own presence. That was a different kind of emptiness, infinitely painful to bear and which she thought could not be worsened until he went away, and she discovered that to be without him altogether exceeded any hurt that she had known before, but must now accept as a burden that she would have to carry with her, since this was a load that she could not lay aside when she left the nursery after the Show, leaving it behind her as she must leave Giles – with Stella – and walk on to face the future alone.

CHAPTER TEN

GILES was laughing the next time Pip saw him, laughing at something Stella said as they parted at the door of the orchid house and the dark-haired girl went inside. He was still smiling, his lips tilted as he turned away, and watching him Pip noticed that his shoulders seemed straighter, his whole bearing looked more confident as he strode towards her. His visit to Stella's people must have been successful after all, she thought dully. She turned towards her own workroom, suddenly unwilling to meet him, afraid to have him close to her, and her heart began to hammer so that her breath was momentarily difficult to come by.

"You sound puffed." He stopped beside her. "Have you been running?"

"What, at this time in the morning?" Flippancy helped. "It's lack of exercise, I expect, I'm out of condition," she slandered her own slight figure.

"Next week should cure that," he prophesied drily. "There'll be enough to do to keep us all in overdrive until the day of the Show. We should be able to relax and enjoy it then, once the display is set up. By the way, how's the layout coming along?" He descended to technicalities, and Pip grasped thankfully at this common ground, forcing her confused mind to follow his questioning and give him the information he sought. With Giles so close to her, her ability to think clearly seemed to disappear.

"George promised Skippy a helicopter ride." Pip gave him all the odds and ends of news she could think of, anything to keep talking, she thought desperately, using conversation as a barrier between herself and the man beside her.

"George spoils her – I'm glad to say." Giles' voice was soft. "I'm glad the wedding's going to be this year, they can all settle down together as a family then."

"You wants to watch it, Mr. Shieldon," one of the women from the packing sheds passed by and heard what he said. "They say weddings always come in threes." She sent him a saucy look, which drew a chuckle from him and a rather weak smile from Pip. Little did the woman know that the second wedding was already imminent. As for the third, she only knew that it wouldn't be hers.

She'd gone off weddings, she decided the following week, standing for a moment outside the spacious tent she and her helpers were busily engaged in laying out for the Show on the following day. The tent next to them had been leased to the local confectionery firms, and from the look of the equipment they were carrying in it seemed that nearly every baker in the neighbourhood had decided to make a wedding cake, Pip thought disgustedly, ignoring the fact that a large part of her own time was occupied in catering for just such functions. She escaped into their own arena, forcing herself to concentrate on the laying out of paths and archways to hold the flowers that they would bring in during the evening ready for the opening of the Show at nine o'clock on the following day. It meant late working, and by the time Pip got back to the cottage dinner was long since past, and she was almost too tired to eat the hot supper that Betsy had kept ready for her return. She saw no sign of Stella, and she didn't expect to, since it was only usually at mealtimes that they met, and for once she was glad to be on her own. She didn't feel like fending off the other girl's barbed remarks tonight. "Let it be a nice day tomorrow," was her last conscious thought before sleep claimed her, and it seemed the dawn chorus was scarcely under way before her alarm clock roused her to run to the window and check on the weather.

It was fine.

A sigh of relief escaped her, and she dressed with luxurious slowness, relishing the fact that this morning, for once, there was no need to hasten to start work. Except for Giles' container of roses, everything was already in place in the tent. The nursery staff were going to attend the shrubs during the day, and would be on duty until the end of the Show, and Giles insisted that Pip take the day off to enjoy herself along with Betsy and her family.

"You can come and help me to cut the roses and display them," he qualified, taking one last look round the tent before they made for home. "You've done well," he approved.

It was a small warmth to take with her and carry her through the day, which she guessed might need all her courage before it ended. Afterwards – tomorrow – she could tell him that she intended to leave the nursery. She would make the excuse that she wanted to move on to further her career. It seemed a cold word for what to Pip was a vocation, but it would do, and it should not to be too difficult to get him to agree. With his marriage to Stella to look forward to, her going would mean nothing more to him than an inconvenience suffered by losing a member of his staff.

The roses must surely be prizewinners, she thought, watching him cut each one carefully from the plot inside the walled garden, making a long stem. He chose only the most perfect buds, moving here and there among his precious bushes until he had sufficient for the container for the tent, and the regulation number for the show bench itself, from which the winners must be chosen.

"Mind the thorns." He handed them over to Pip to hold while he shut his knife blade and returned the tool to his pocket. "Well? Will they do?" His voice and eyes were soft, and he smiled as Pip surfaced from burying her face in their heady fragrance.

"They're perfect!"

"Let's hope the judges think so." He took her arm and turned her towards the gate in the wall. "It's time we were off. We'll carry them loose and arrange them when we get there."

She collected the container in which they were to stand, and got into the car beside Giles, the roses resting on tissue paper in a box on her knee, and looked her surprise when he started the engine straight away.

"Where's Stella? Has she gone on with the others?" She couldn't imagine the other girl condescending to travel with the foreman in the station wagon, unless Giles had specifically told her to. It would be completely out of character.

"She's having a lie in," Giles retorted. "It's going to be a long day for all of us, and as we're not showing orchids ... she's coming along later," he added absentmindedly, his attention on the turning out of the nursery gates into the lane.

If I'd been going to marry Giles, thought Pip angrily, I'd have got up and gone with him whatever time in the morning the Show started. Stella seemed to have no thought for anyone else but herself, not even for the man she was going to marry. If he won he would want his fiancée to be there to share the glory with him, and if he did not get the prize, she could at least be there to console him, she criticised silently.

"Ouch!"

Her angry thoughts were terminated abruptly by an incautious grasp of one of the roses, which promptly retaliated and drew blood by a particularly vicious thorn.

"I told you to mind them." Giles removed the bloom from her finger and took hold of the rose himself, pushing it expertly into its place in the container. "That's all for this one, the rest are for the show bench." He put the others aside. "Is it much?" he asked sympathetically, grasping her hand and turning it palm upwards so that he could see where her finger still oozed blood.

"It'll soon stop." Pip pressed her thumb against it, burningly conscious of his touch.

"Mind not to get it on your trouser suit, it'll mark." He referred to the sunshine yellow crimplene suit which, teamed with a white silk sweater and white pumps, seemed an ideal combination for a warm summer day on the showground. Pip stuffed her other hand into her pocket and drew out a paper handkerchief.

"This'll do." She wound it round carelessly, and turned with a relief that she hoped did not show as Skippy raced through the tent entrance calling for their attention.

"Come and see," she tugged at Pip's jacket excitedly, "there's some baby calves, an' some Shetland ponies, an' some big woolly teddy bears," she spread her arms wide to indicate their size.

"Not all in one pen?" gasped Pip, and turned as George's deep chuckle answered her from behind.

"What a scramble if they were," he laughed. "No, the woolly teddy bears are on the Women's Institute handicraft stall," he pointed in the opposite direction. "The calves are on the stock side, over there, and I don't know about the ponies. I expect they'll be in the buggy races later on," he hoped.

"I know where they are, I've seen them. Come and look," the youngster begged, and Pip gave in.

"What time do you want her back for the helicopter ride? Are you still going up?" She wondered if George might have changed his mind; he was a fairly stolid individual normally, and inclined to keep his feet firmly on the ground, metaphorically if not physically.

"Oh yes, we're all going up. It's a bit of a treat, like, to celebrate," he looked confused.

172

"What an unusual idea!" Pip enthused with him. The whole family were so patently happy with the coming wedding that it was difficult not to feel glad with them.

"Bring her back when you're ready, we're stopping here all day so there's plenty of time," the foreman retorted. "And in the meantime, just be good!" He directed a firm look in Skippy's direction. He spoiled her outrageously, but he obviously had no illusions, and she nodded solemnly.

"I'll look after Pip." She slid her small paw responsibly into Pip's, who tried with reasonable success to keep a straight face. She felt Giles' grin behind their retreating backs, and gave herself up to her small guide's directions.

"What are we going to see first?"

"The ponies." Skippy was quite decided, and wriggled her hand free to run on ahead, while Pip followed at a more leisurely pace, reluctant to disturb the feeling of relaxation at being in the middle of a host of interesting happenings, and having a whole day free to enjoy them. She joined Skippy at the side of the roped-in enclosure ahead. The ropes, she noticed with amusement, were not to keep the animals in so much as to keep the public out. A couple of feet inside the ropes was a temporary stockade, effective in keeping the little Shetland ponies confined, and Pip watched beside Skippy, delighted at the miniature herd that wandered round the arena awaiting their turn to perform, occasionally giving a naughty buck.

"It's sheer showing off," she laughed, and the small girl turned a bright face up to hers.

"I like that one best. He bites." She pointed to a mischievous-looking pony in a corner of the arena that had a wicked look in its eye, of which the other animals were obviously aware, for Pip noticed several of them gave it a wide berth.

"That's not very nice," she began, and a belegginged

man on the other side of the fence looked across at them.

"He's got real spirit, that one," he told them proudly, "though to handle he's a right little . . . hmmm!" He recollected the child's presence just in time, and busied himself rubbing the curry-comb in his hand down the leg of his cords.

"I see you've roped us out," Pip digressed hastily.

"We 'as to, miss." He looked relieved. "It's surprising 'ow many folk thinks of animals as dustbins," he told her indignantly. "They sees one on t'other side of a fence, and stuffs it with all sorts. Apples, sandwiches, chocolate – the wrappings too, sometimes," he complained with such a near replica of Sam's growl that both Pip and Skippy stifled a giggle. "Then they gets colic, and I 'as a night up." He sounded aggrieved.

"I didn't know ponies got tummyache." As a veteran eater of green apples, Skippy knew all about tummy-aches.

"See that you don't!" Her mother and Betsy appeared through the crowd and issued a timely warning. "No sweeties unless you ask first," she told her daughter.

"Uncle George said I could have two ice creams, one 'smorning and one 'safternoon," Skippy protested, with an expression of one whose future suddenly looks grey and unattractive.

"They won't hurt you," her grandmother relented, "but don't have one before you go up in that helicopter thing, have it after," she added, wise in the ways of small interiors, if not of the peculiar-looking aircraft that even now was circling to land and take on its first load of passengers for a joy-ride round the grounds. It settled close to them, and Skippy's face became vivid with excitement, ice creams and ponies and all else forgotten in this new, strange mode of transport that previously she had only seen on the television screen.

"Let's go and see," she tugged the grown-ups' hands pleadingly.

"We're close enough." Her mother took a firm grasp of the seat of her dungarees, and held on. "I don't know as George did the right thing. ...." she said worriedly, eyeing the whirling rotor blades from which the wind could be felt even from where they stood.

"Of course he did. It'll be a wonderful experience, you'll see." Giles joined them and added a reassuring voice to Skippy's protests that she wanted to go up even if her mother didn't. "I thought of persuading Pip to go along with you," he teased. George had evidently told him of her refusal beforehand, the twinkle in his eye dared her to change her mind.

"No fear!" she retorted, vexed at being pressured when she had already said "no". "I'll wave to you from the ground," she tossed the gauntlet back, and he chuckled. Away from the nursery and its many calls on his time and attention he could be warmly human, she found, a re-alisation that had come to her at the ball at the Manor Hotel, and she wished suddenly that she had not known this side of him; it did not make her dilemma any the easier to bear. If she could have remembered him as the curt, unapproachable being she first knew as her em-ployer, it would have been easy. But then she would not have had to leave the nursery, she reflected, and sighed, her spirits dropping.

"It's too long since you had breakfast," Giles spotted the effect even if he wrongly diagnosed the cause. "Let's have a picnic," he suggested boyishly, "and if George doesn't turn up we'll start without him," he said in a conspiratorial tone that brought a giggle of mischief from Skippy, who plainly hoped her future stepfather would find them all replete when he eventually arrived. The band from the County regiment struck up a brisk tune as a preliminary to their display of counter-marching, and roused them from the grass after their meal was done.

"That drum's too close for comfort." Giles rubbed his

ear ruefully. "Let's move on," he suggested. "They'll sound better from a distance."

"We've been having a look at the wedding cakes in the tent next to ours. Have you seen them, miss?" Skippy's mother looked wistful, and Pip hoped that someone would have enough forethought to provide a nice one for her. After years of hardship, it would at least be a good omen to start her new life. Perhaps the nursery staff would have a whip-round. She shelved the idea temporarily, but let it lie in her mind. George could not suggest such a thing, neither could Betsy or Sam, so it would really be up to herself or Stella. She would have a word with the forewoman in the packing shed, she decided; it would not matter that she herself would not be there to see to the collection, once the idea took hold it would carry on by its own momentum, and she could leave her own donation with one of the staff.

"I haven't seen them yet," she answered gently. "I watched them carrying the stands in last night while we were working on our own display, but I haven't got around to inspecting the cakes themselves."

"Let's go now." Giles took her by the arm. "I've got to go back to our own tent anyway to see that all's well there, and we can do the round from there," he suggested.

Pip couldn't very well refuse, though the last thing she felt she wanted was to see a display of wedding cakes, particularly in Giles' company. Weddings were something that for today at any rate she felt she wanted to forget.

"You're a craftsman, John." Healthy respect tinged Giles' voice as he spoke to their local baker, complacently viewing his largest creation that to Pip's awed eyes must have taken ages to perfect. It was a square cake, which Pip liked, the simple, clean lines attracting her, as did the lack of artificial decoration.

"You've chosen roses, too." She eyed the delicate cascade of icing sugar rosebuds that dropped from the top tier to the other three below so naturally that they might well have been scattered there by some careless hand, each tier carrying buds that were slightly more open than the one before, until they ended in two single blooms on the silver board on which it stood, each flushed so faintly pink that the colouring was hardly noticeable. Incredibly fine icing filigree work was the cake's only other decoration, but done with such a masterful hand that the whole effect of the four-tier cake was one of airy lightness, a work of art indeed.

"Skippy's mother said she liked the one with the bride and groom on the top." Giles' eyes roved across the table seeking her choice.

"Ah well, we have to cater for every taste, Mr. Shieldon," the baker replied. "This one's a great favourite with a lot of the ladies." He indicated one with the top tier carrying a miniature china bride and groom, with the names of the happy couple inscribed on the side of the bottom tier, and more conservative decorations adorning the other two. To Pip it looked overdressed, though it was undoubtedly cleverly done, and some of her thoughts must have shown on her face, for the baker smiled.

"I fancy you like this one," he indicated the other. "I do too," he confided, "my best work's gone into that."

"Can you do another one like this?" Giles waved his hand at the one supporting the happy couple. "We've got a wedding at the nursery, and it would make them a nice present. What do you think?" he turned to Pip.

"Oh, I was hoping someone would. . . ." Pip stopped, wondering if she should have spoken, and Giles looked at her keenly.

"You noticed what Skippy's mum said, too," he commented softly. "I thought you had, you looked at her fairly hard at the time."

"She sounded so wistful." Pip felt quite choky at the thought.

"Then we'll settle on one like this for her, how will that do? It'll not be until the autumn, John," he told the baker, "so you'll have plenty of time, if you'll oblige?"

"That I will, and gladly, Mr. Shieldon. Though I'd be happier still if it was for yourself," he said forthrightly, and Pip felt herself go hot as the baker's kindly eyes rested on her with a twinkle.

"Ah yes, as to that . . . well, you never know, I might be ordering two instead of one," Giles retorted with an enigmatic smile, but he gave no definite commitment. He could hardly do so, Pip realised. That would be up to Stella's people, and her local baker, presumably somewhere near London. Did the parents of a divorcee provide a second reception? she wondered. It was a point she had not thought of before, but if they didn't Giles would no doubt see that Stella had whatever party she desired for the occasion. It would probably be held in some fashionable, chromium-plated restaurant, guessed Pip, thinking longingly of the rooms at the Manor Hotel, that still retained the gracious beauty of another age, and lent it to the functions that were held there. Giles fitted naturally into such a setting, but to Stella it was alien. She did not belong, and even as Giles' wife she still would not fit in, probably wouldn't want to, guessed Pip, for Stella seemed to scorn most of the accepted values, rejecting established ways for devious paths of her own, along which Giles' feet would shortly have to follow, though thinking of Stella's first disastrous attempt at marriage Pip wondered for how long they would eventually travel together. To the end? Or would they lose their footing half way in the same mire in which her previous marriage had foundered? For Giles' sake Pip hoped that all would go well. She loved him too much to want him to face the emptiness of disillusion that she feared would leave him an embittered recluse. His tendency to solitude would not help him, she guessed, regretting the potential waste that it was not in her power to prevent.

"These must be the woolly teddy bears Skippy's been on about." Pip stopped fascinated beside the next display, which combined a selection of every conceivable craft the area could produce, from intricate wood carving to the toy-making section that, from the interested audience crowded about the stall, appealed to children from six to sixty.

"And they call these home crafts," murmured Giles, as interested as Pip.

"The standard's professional," she agreed. "I love that one, don't you?" She pointed to a miniature bear in a pale cream colour, with dark chocolate ears and paws. "Oh, look!" Her face lit up with delight. "He's got patches on his pants the same colour as his paws!" A small child, unable to see enough for his liking, tugged at the cloth covering the table, and the tiny teddy bear toppled on to its face, revealing the patches on its nether regions that brought a smile to the face of every grown-up watching.

"Let's take him along with us," suggested Giles seriously, rejecting the offer of a bag from the amused stallholder. "We want his company," he smiled, and callously swung his new acquisition upside down by his heels.

"He'll get better treatment from Skippy," Pip rebuked him, and Giles gave her a quizzical look.

"Will he, now?" he murmured, but when Skippy raced up to them with George and her mother in tow, to Pip's surprise he made no move to give her the toy, although he held it out for her to see.

"Isn't he nice?" Skippy stroked the brown ears. "Uncle George gave me the one next to him. Mine's pink," she voiced her sympathy that Giles' bear was not of the same rosy hue. "Mummy's put mine in her bag, 'cos he doesn't like flying," she told him gravely.

"I fancy you've not averse to keeping him company," murmured Giles sotto voce as they fell in beside Skippy's mother, with George and the excited child leading the way to the helicopter landing area.

"That I'm not," their companion admitted forthrightly. "Skippy chose this one," she held him up for their inspection. "Pink's her favourite colour just now. I told her he'd turn green with fright if he went up in that thing," she added unrepentantly, indicating the helicopter which was just disgorging its latest load of passengers. "George said he reckoned the bear was too young to be left on his own, and that convinced her. It let me off going up with them," she finished with relief.

"Thoughtful George!" Pip scored another point in the foreman's favour.

"I dunno as I likes them going up, either." She eyed her daughter and her husband-to-be, who had stopped at the side of the helicopter to wave to her before they disappeared inside.

"They'll be quite safe," comforted Giles. "Wave back to them, they're just off," he urged, giving her something to do as the machine rose above their heads. He gave Pip a significant look, and took the older woman's arm.

"Come with us, we're just going to watch them unload the show jumpers," he coaxed, clearly unwilling to let her remain on her own and worry until the helicopter should return. The fifteen minutes' joy flight would seem like fifteen years to her, thought Pip sympathetically, and felt grateful that Giles had the perception to see this, and the consideration to do something about it. It was news to her that she and Giles were going to see the horses unloaded, but she followed willingly enough, glad to do her share, for she had formed an affection for her landlady and her family. She would miss them all when she left.

Two horseboxes had already drawn to a halt and were

disgorging their occupants, perfectly groomed mares in tip-top condition, who seemed quite unruffled by their confined quarters, and backed down the ramps on to the grass with a quiet lack of fuss, from where they eyed the admiring crowd about them as if they were already confident of their own success in the coming afternoon's events.

"Why, look, there's Miss Garvey," Skippy's mother pointed to the other side of the horseboxes.

"I can't see. . . ."

"You can now, just in front of that man in the yellow sweater."

The bright splash of colour placed Stella, and Pip waved to attract her attention, but she did not respond.

"I'll go and fetch her, she might as well join us if she's staying." Giles left them and made his way through the crowd towards the other girl.

"He don't sound too keen," observed Skippy's mother shrewdly, and Pip hid her own surprise at his remark. Maybe Betsy and her family were not as yet aware of the attachment between the two, and it was not her place to enlighten them. She knew the news would not be welcome to the little family, who had Giles' interests as much at heart as their own, but she felt it could keep. Giles would take them into his confidence when he was ready, and not until.

Stella herself already looked bored, her eyes searching the ground, probably seeking Giles, and the look on her face making it evident that she could find a dozen things to do which would better interest her. Giles must have called to her, for she turned round, and instantly her face brightened. She took a couple of steps towards Giles, fumbling with her handbag, and as they came close she extricated what looked like a long white envelope, and handed it to him. He spoke to her briefly, and ran his thumb under the flap, splitting it open. It couldn't have been a very long letter, but it must have contained very good news, for Giles seemed immediately electrified. He took Stella's shoulders under his arm and pulled her close to him, urging her to read the letter too, while he did the same for the second time, and they smiled at each other as their eyes took in the printed message. Could it be news of Stella's divorce? Was she free at last? She must be. Giles' reaction decided Pip. He behaved in a way that was completely out of character with his usual reserve in public, and flung his arms about the dark-haired girl and kissed her soundly on both cheeks, to the obvious delight of the onlookers.

"Mind, Miss Pip, let's move over a bit. This horse looks a bit scary to me." Skippy's mother eyed the animal coming out of the third loosebox with the same look she had bent on the helicopter, which was even now heading towards them, back towards its landing, the brief flight almost over.

Pip scarcely heard her. The scene she had just witnessed was imprinted on her mind, the shock of it making her numb, and she neither felt nor saw her companion leave her side for the greater safety of distance between herself and the trailer. The helicopter made a slow approach, losing height rapidly, its rotors clattering noisily in the warm air, mocking her misery. It swooped lower, preparatory to landing a few yards away, and as it passed overhead a scuffle exploded on the ground.

"Miss Pip!"

She heard the older woman scream, had time to feel fear as the reason for the scuffle dawned on her, then the high, golden hindquarters of a frightened mare, terrified at the sudden clatter above it, bore down on her, wicked hooves lashing at a danger that was no longer there. Pip stood petrified, fear taking the use from her limbs so that she was unable to move, then a pair of hard arms grabbed her, swung her off her feet that were having difficulty in supporting her anyway, swung her high as if she was no heavier than Skippy's slight weight, and put her down gently a safe distance from the now subdued, but still trembling mare.

"Is she all right, sir?" It was one of the grooms, and he was shaking the arm of her rescuer anxiously.

"Yes, she wasn't touched, only frightened. I'll look after her." It was Giles' voice, Giles' arm that was about her, that had plucked her away from the danger at the risk of getting hurt himself. Somewhere in the daze that held her Pip realised she ought to thank him. She looked up to speak, and her words choked at the light on his face. Momentarily she had forgotten the letter Stella had given to him. The joy of the news it contained was still there, lighting his eyes as if the familiar shadows that had darkened them from when she first knew him had never been.

"You've dropped your letter, Mr. Giles." Skippy's mother retrieved it from the grass where it had fallen when he grabbed Pip.

"Oh, thanks," he took it from her. "It's marvellous news, the very best," he told Pip, and spontaneously his arms tightened about her. "Now I can ask you. . . ." he began.

"Mr. Giles!" It was George, running towards them, with Skippy hard on his heels. "Mr. Giles, they're judging the roses. You must come, gaffer," he was breathless from his haste.

"You were going to ask?" Pip didn't know what he had been going to ask. Perhaps that she should look after things, as she had done before, while he and Stella were away on their honeymoon.

"I'll ask you later." He bent his head so that George should not hear, and still keeping one arm about her shoulders, and the other grasping the arm of Skippy's mother to help her to hurry along with them, he followed his foreman back towards the competition stand, and the container of his precious blooms.

"Isn't Stella coming?" Pip had lost sight of her in the

excitement, but surely she must be with Giles when they announced the results of the rose entries. "Shall we wait?" She dragged back, looking round for Stella in the crowd.

"It's no use waiting for Stella, she's gone home." Giles was impatient, pulling her with him. "She's expecting a phone call from her husband. She's had some good news as well," he told her casually.

So her guess had been correct; the divorce had gone through.

"He'll be able to take her with him after all," Giles carried on talking when the queue for the helicopter rides temporarily blocked their path, and he had to steady his haste for a moment. "He was going on an orchid-hunting trip abroad. It was arranged before he and Stella decided to have another go at making their marriage work, and he wasn't able to take her along, so she had to be content to wave him off from London."

"London? That's when you both went. . . ." Pip's mind seemed to return to its daze, and she felt like pinching herself to see if she was really awake.

"Yes, I went to see our M.P., so I told Stella she might as well travel down with me and save her rail fare, the same as she did at Easter. But to get back to her husband, it seems one of his party on this trip has had to drop out. He was taken ill when they were only two days out, so Stella can take his place. It's funny," he said reflectively, "I never connected Stella with Alan Mitchell before."

"You know her husband?" It got stranger and stranger, thought Pip bemusedly.

"Yes, but when Stella came to the nursery she used her maiden name of Garvey. It was quite by chance that I met up with Alan. You remember," he reminded her, "it was that day I took you in to the Manor Hotel. The one when that sports car driver nearly sent us both to our ancestors." His tone was briefly grim, betraying the shock of the near miss. "Well, her husband was in the bar waiting for his meal to be served, so we decided to eat together. I knew him years ago, when we were both at college," he explained. "To cut a long story short, Stella came into the dining room with one of her – er – escorts," his tone indicated his opinion of the escort, and probably of Stella, Pip realised with a growing sense of unreality. "Alan Mitchell is a fairly determined man," he smiled reminiscently, "and he decided it was time he took a firm hand. It seems to have worked," he grinned suddenly. "I persuaded Stella to leave her escort and join us for the meal, and the rest you probably know."

Pip didn't. Stella had never confided in her, always treating Pip as the intruder she had considered her to be when she first joined the staff, but there was no point in telling Giles all this now. There was no time anyway, the queue was moving on, there was a gap in the crowd, and Giles tugged her forward again towards the exhibition benches. Suddenly life took on a new dimension for Pip. The cheerful crowd, intent on enjoying their day; the purposeful noise and bustle about them took on a sharp clarity, and the sunshine, that before had merely made her feel hot, now seemed something to glory in. Giles no longer had to help her to keep up with his long strides. She ran happily beside him, though she was breathless when they reached a halt beside the stand containing their own roses. The judging had already begun, and the Lord Mayor was even then announcing the third prize winner.

"Miller's Nurseries – congratulations, Mr. Miller." He handed over a small silver cup, and shook the hand of the man receiving it, who made way for the second prize winner coming up behind him. "Mr. Pedlar of Mossly – congratulations to you." Another cup changed hands, and Pip held her breath. Who would be next? She felt Giles tense beside her, knew the agony of the moment with him as his hand reached for hers, reached and held it tightly, and she put her other hand to it, cupping his fingers between her own small palms, willing him to feel her support, and by his tightening grip she knew he did.

"The winner of the first prize, the winner of the rose bowl, is a brand new rose that until now has had no name." The Lord Mayor smiled at Giles' upturned face at the foot of the steps. "The first prize goes to Mr. Giles Shieldon, of Shieldon's Rose Nurseries," he announced, and gestured to Giles to join him on the stand. Pip wriggled her fingers to free them from his grasp, but instead he tightened it, drawing her with him up the steps, one by one beside him until they reached the top, and he had to loose her hand then to receive the beautifully chased silver rose bowl from the hands of the Lady Mayoress. "And now I have a very pleasant task to perform," the Mayor raised his hand for silence that at last brought the applause to a reluctant end. There was no doubt that it was a popular "first" among the local people. "I'm given leave by Mr. Shieldon to name his new rose – step aside, Giles, so that everyone can see." He herded Pip and Giles from in front of their entry to a ripple of laughter from the onlookers, and drew aside a piece of white silk that Pip had thought merely covered the base of the container. Giles turned her round so that she, too, could see what it revealed, a plain white card with bold black lettering, that announced the name of his prize-winning rose, the culmination of his long held dream.

"Philippa."

"The rose is almost as lovely as its namesake."

There was no mistaking the meaning of the Lord Mayor's words, or his significant bow towards the slight figure in yellow standing at Giles' side, and this time there was no stopping the applause.

"Give me a picture, Mr. Shieldon?"

It was the young reporter, and Giles obligingly held up the rose bowl for him, while his camera flashed.

"Now give me the one I want," the newspaper man

said with an impish grin, and Pip gasped as Giles' arms went about her, drawing her close, encircling her as she had so often longed for them to do, and despite the crowd she did not draw away. This was where she belonged, and this was where she would stay. And now there was no need for her to hide from him the expression in her eyes as they looked into his, and read the question that was in them only for her.

"You said you could ask me now. Why now?" She smiled up at him mischievously, and his eyes lightened in response.

"I couldn't ask you to marry me before." Momentarily the familiar shadow returned to his face. "I didn't know if I'd be able to offer you a home, if the road went through the nursery. I had to wait. . . ." The darkness in his eyes told Pip how much the waiting had meant to him. "Now I needn't wait any longer." He waved the letter that Stella had given to him. "This is from our M.P. He says they're decided on routing the new road across the edge of the common;" he told her thankfully, "so Shieldon's is safe – if you'll stay?"

"I'll stay," it was only a whisper, but it sufficed to chase the shadows away from his eyes, and bring back the gaiety that would always have its place there so long as Pip was by his side.

"Let's take him home, shall we?" He perched the small teddy bear in the middle of the rose bowl for convenience of carrying them both. "I bought him for us," he told Pip gravely. "I reckoned we might have a use for him later on. . . ."

Have you missed any of these bestselling Harlequin Romances?

Please use the attached order form to indicate your requirements. All titles are available at 75¢ each. Offer expires March 31/77.

Please use the attached order form to indicate your requirements. All titles are available at 75¢ each. Offer expires March 31/77.

Harlequin Reader Service
ORDER FORM

MAIL COUPON TO ➤ Harlequin Reader Service, M.P.O. Box 707, Niagara Falls, New York 14302.

Canadian SEND Residents TO: ➤ Harlequin Reader Service, Stratford, Ont. N5A 6W4

―――――――――――――――――――――――――

〉 **A HARLEQUIN ROMANCE** 〈

Please check novels requested:

☐ 901	☐ 931	☐ 1025	☐ 1228	☐ 1369	☐ 1400	☐ 1415
☐ 904	☐ 932	☐ 1026	☐ 1230	☐ 1370	☐ 1401	☐ 1417
☐ 905	☐ 967	☐ 1030	☐ 1266	☐ 1373	☐ 1402	☐ 1418
☐ 907	☐ 973	☐ 1036	☐ 1274	☐ 1374	☐ 1403	☐ 1419
☐ 911	☐ 977	☐ 1044	☐ 1354	☐ 1376	☐ 1404	☐ 1421
☐ 913	☐ 985	☐ 1048	☐ 1356	☐ 1377	☐ 1406	☐ 1422
☐ 915	☐ 1004	☐ 1107	☐ 1357	☐ 1378	☐ 1407	☐ 1425
☐ 918	☐ 1005	☐ 1109	☐ 1358	☐ 1379	☐ 1410	☐ 1429
☐ 920	☐ 1006	☐ 1117	☐ 1360	☐ 1381	☐ 1411	☐ 1505
☐ 924	☐ 1011	☐ 1122	☐ 1362	☐ 1386	☐ 1412	
☐ 925	☐ 1013	☐ 1125	☐ 1364	☐ 1387	☐ 1413	
☐ 927	☐ 1019	☐ 1136	☐ 1366	☐ 1389	☐ 1414	

Please send me by return mail the books which I have checked.
I am enclosing 75¢ for each book ordered.

Number of books ordered _____ @ 75¢ each = $ _____

Postage and Handling = .25

TOTAL = $ _____

Name _____

Address _____

City _____

State/Prov. _____

Zip/Postal Code _____

Harlequin Presents...

BY POPULAR DEMAND . . .

36 original novels from this series -- by 3 of the world's greatest romance authors.

These back issues by Anne Hampson, Anne Mather, and Violet Winspear have been out of print for some time. So don't miss out, order your copies now!

All the above titles are available at 95¢ each. Please use the attached order form to indicate your requirements.

Offer expires March 31, 1977

Harlequin Reader Service

ORDER FORM

MAIL COUPON TO ➤ Harlequin Reader Service,
M.P.O. Box 707,
Niagara Falls, New York 14302.

Canadian SEND Residents TO: ➤ Harlequin Reader Service,
Stratford, Ont. N5A 6W4

Harlequin Presents...

Please check Volumes requested:

☐ 1	☐ 2	☐ 3	☐ 4	☐ 5
☐ 7	☐ 8	☐ 9	☐ 10	☐ 11
☐ 12	☐ 13	☐ 14	☐ 15	☐ 16
☐ 17	☐ 18	☐ 19	☐ 20	☐ 21
☐ 22	☐ 23	☐ 24	☐ 25	☐ 26
☐ 27	☐ 28	☐ 29	☐ 30	☐ 31
☐ 32	☐ 33	☐ 34	☐ 35	☐ 36
☐ 37				

Please send me by return mail the books which I have checked.
I am enclosing 95¢ for each book ordered.

Number of books ordered_____ @ 95¢ each = $ _____

Postage and Handling = .25

TOTAL = $ _____

Name _____

Address _____

City _____

State/Prov. _____

Zip/Postal Code _____